MAKING IT WHILE Faking IT

THE LORDS OF MANHATTAN

ZOEY LOCKE
Z.L. ARKADIE

Exit Stage Left

TREASURE GROVE

That was brutal.

The pressure in my head builds toward explosion as I flee the live set where an actual TV show is being filmed. Several of my emotions battle each other for the top spot. I'm embarrassed, angry, fed up with this whole ordeal, and plain old sad. Pinching the bridge of my nose, I force the tears that want to come gushing from my eyes to stay put. I refuse to give Liam Caruso, our jerk director, the satisfaction of knowing he made me cry. He's been on a mission to break me ever since day one, and maybe he finally has. It's too soon to tell.

The morning air is chilly, but storming off the set generated a lot of body heat, so I'm too hot to feel the cold. I'm walking so fast that I'm practically running. I glance over my shoulder. The makeshift wooden wall built around a dirt pit that's supposed to be the inside of medieval manor is in the distance. Finally, I'm far enough from the scene of the crime to slow my pace and catch my breath.

"The horses are famished, Father—are you certain they can take the journey?" I whisper in the accented voice of my character.

I have such a horrible English accent. And damn it—it's "make the journey," not "take the journey."

I stop at the edge of a wooden floor built between two long rows of star trailers and lift my face to the opaque gray overcast. My eyes flicker closed as I groan in misery. In my head, I hear my dad's voice asking if I'm ready to take any responsibility for Caruso blowing up and kicking me off the set.

"Okay," I whisper against a refreshingly mild wind. I messed up my lines.

Before botching "make," I said "Mother" instead of "Father." And before that, I said "hamished," which isn't even a real word, instead of "famished."

A wave of nausea overcomes me, and I groan as I bend over and grab my knees. Breathing deeply, I really concentrate to keep down the bagel and cup of black coffee I had for breakfast this morning. I wasn't hungry. I haven't been that hungry since arriving in Iceland. As soon as the airplane landed and after a foreboding helicopter ride over fields of desolate glaciers, I lost my appetite. I don't want to be here. I never even wanted the part in this new TV show, which is sure to be a flop, but I certainly need the part.

I squeeze my eyes shut and pinch the bridge of my nose again. *Don't cry, Treas.* Thinking about my misery and what's at stake if I don't finish out my obligation to this television show always makes me want to bawl like a baby.

The sobering truth is that I'm not a good actress. I also own up to that fact that I would've never landed the role of Raylene Preen, the king's favorite daughter who will eventually get her head sliced clean off in episode four, if it weren't for the worst kind of nepotism. I'm engaged to internationally famous actor Simon Linney, and it's because of him that I got the role. That's why everybody around here thinks I'm a spoiled heiress who's making a mockery of their thespian profession. And nobody thinks that more than Caruso. But I am by no means spoiled or rich, not anymore at least. It's been the better part of ten years since I received any money from the family trust.

I sigh as I stop pinching the bridge of my nose. It's time to think my way out of my mere definition of hell on earth. I was on the verge of ending things with Simon before he proposed I take a part in *Marked by the Sword*, thereby ending my cash flow problem. I bought a restaurant. I made it popular. One would think that popularity meant making a lot of money, but that's not true in my case. I'm approximately one month away from being forced to close the doors of my restaurant, The Chest of Chelsea. Everything is expensive to maintain in my restaurant, even Nya Jones, the real reason why my restaurant has become so popular. She's a high-priced celebrity chef that I hired to be my head chef.

Although Simon landed me my current gig, my contract is with Jaycee Wilding, the executive producer. I have no more than five lines total, but so far, all the trailer promos have included images of me, Treasure Grove, as Raylene Preen. They want my twenty-six million social media followers, the bulk of which I acquired before opening my restaurant, to watch their show.

My social media followers are foodies in their late twenties and thirties, and these people are the movie's target audience. So far, I have been paid one of the three million dollars owed to me for my role as Raylene Preen. I used that money to keep my restaurant afloat for the remainder of this month. I'll be paid another one million upon completion of my last performance, which is supposed to be next Friday if there are no more scheduling delays. Liam Caruso has a problem with time management. Regardless, that money will float my restaurant for another month. My final payment is to be released no more than twenty-four hours after the pilot episode is aired, given that I have made the seventy-five posts touting *Marked by the Sword* to my social media followers. I've already hired someone to do that.

"But I can make Jaycee a better deal," I whisper.

I have many famous friends with millions upon millions of social media followers. I can ask them to post about the television show as a favor to me. But first, she's going to have to double my pay and cut my time in Iceland short. "Like today," I say to the chilly air that's making me colder by the second. I want to be out of this godforsaken hellhole with its twiggy fields of wild grass and nothing to see but prairie land for miles on out.

I sigh with dread as my fiancé's face fills my head. I'll have to persuade Simon to let me go.

In the end, he has all the power. If he tells Jaycee to tell me to fuck off, then she'll say in her unaffected businesslike voice, "Treasure, I'm sorry, but you will have to fuck off." Because in these parts, the big star, Simon Linney, the fiancé I probably should've never said yes to, the man I really want to break up with, has all the power. And Simon can be a capricious and selfish prick.

So I cross my fingers and look up at the sky. Blue is breaking through the white clouds. Maybe that's a good sign.

Eyes lifted high in prayer, I say, "Give me luck, God. Please, get me out of this desolate prairie."

Just When I Need Him

TREASURE GROVE

Fists balled and ready to knock on the door of Simon's luxurious trailer, I fill my lungs with the untainted, crisp Iceland air, preparing myself to break the news to him. Tomorrow at this time, I want to be waking up in my bed back in New York City.

Out of nowhere, a thought flashes through my mind. I wonder if I'd be so miserable here if I had the same accommodations as Simon. My trailer is shoebox sized. Water barely trickles out of the faucet, the toilet barely flushes, and the bed feels like I'm sleeping on wood. But that's not the case for Simon, who has the largest and most luxurious trailer on the lot. I thought he and I were supposed to live together, but according to

Jaycee, that's not allowed. She explained, clearly lying but with a straight face that he's the main star and privacy is needed for purposes of confidentiality. I knew then that Simon put her up to telling me that, but I made myself believe what she said. Now, I'm no longer willing to delude myself. Yes, Simon is seriously a selfish prick. And yes, I agreed to marry him, but I knew deep down in my bones that I would never go through with it.

I don't know what time it is because I'm not wearing a watch and my cell phone is in my trailer, but my guess is that it's only minutes before or after eight a.m. Simon should be asleep. He spent all day yesterday on set. He's not supposed to shoot again until early tomorrow morning. He works hard practicing his lines and performing them to perfection. He really is a great actor who needs his rest. I glance nervously over my shoulder, wondering if I should just go back to my trailer and give him a few more hours of undisturbed peace. I shake my leg anxiously, appearing as though I have to pee. The thing is… I can't wait, because this is an emergency.

I pull my fist back to knock, but I stop. I hear a noise inside the trailer. It's definitely Simon's voice. He's awake? But there's something about the sound he made that puts my ears on high alert. My expression is tight. Then there's another sound. It's muffled, but it's definitely made by a woman.

I snap back, leaning away from the door. "What the…" I whisper.

Okay, so…

It's true. Simon Linney is notorious for being a cheater. But I allowed him to convince me that those days of banging every beautiful woman he meets are far behind him. "Only immature boys cheat. I'm a real man, Treasure, and men are loyal," he had said in his smart and rather convincing English accent. I shake my head, hoping to be wrong about what I suspect. I say a little prayer—if I'm wrong, then I'll take it as a sign to do whatever it takes to make our relationship work.

I twist my lips thoughtfully as my body processes the declaration I just made.

Maybe not.

But first things first—I carefully grab the door's lever and crank it downward. I close my eyes as I sigh with relief. It's unlocked.

My heart beats like thunder as I glance quickly but thoroughly over my right and then left shoulders. The coast is still clear. Fueled by the unmistakable sound of a woman's faint giggle, I carefully pull the door toward me and hurriedly step inside.

The stark difference of the indoor temperature from the outside makes me shiver as my blood heats up. I wish I could enjoy the pleasant warmth wafting across my face. Suddenly, I remember that I'm wearing my heavy, ugly, wild-looking faux-fur dress. The material makes my skin itch, but I can't scratch. I have to remain quiet. Rule number one—catch him in the act, see with my own eyes. Then he can't lie.

I hear the bed creaking, slurping, and a lustful "Yes, Cherry baby, like that."

My eyes grow wide, and I can't stop shaking my head. Holy shit, he's getting blown. And Cherry? Is it Cherry Attwell, the second-biggest star on set, who's licking his stick? Yes—it has to be her. She's the only Cherry out here.

The traitorous bitch.

I strongly dislike girls who spit in the face of the girl code.

In my mind's eye, I see her face as she sits with me and Simon in his trailer, joining us for coffee some mornings, dinner some evenings, and the small cocktail party Simon threw the other night. Cherry's playing his love interest, who is the daughter of our family's rival clan. Even with all their sexual tension during scenes, I don't think I ever noticed anything genuinely sexual between them. Or had I? Had I been so blinded by my need to keep my restaurant afloat that I looked away when their stares lingered for too long or she brushed against him as he stood at the sink?

I pad up the narrow hallway that leads to a master suite that rivals any five-star hotel room. I grimace, palm against my stomach as the unmistakable scent of sex taints the air and makes me nauseous.

"There, you're hard. Let's fuck," Cherry says as if they've done what they're doing a million times before and it's time for the next step.

The sound of Simon sipping air between his teeth is sharp and laced with longing. I can also tell that he's trying very hard to keep his sex sounds quiet. He doesn't want anyone to hear him, especially me.

He won't hear me, though. My steps are expertly silent as I inch closer to the doorway like a stalking lioness. I take two final steps and then carefully flatten my back against the wall. I lean forward, inch by inch, until I'm able to see them. They're both so into what they're doing that neither has felt my presence. Simon is naked as a jaybird and is on his knees, positioned between Cherry's pencil-thin legs.

"Spread them wider," Simon commands gruffly as he strokes himself.

Oh, that's right, he loves barking out commands during sex.

"Wider," he orders.

He'll keep telling her to spread her thighs until her joints ache and her legs quiver.

But my eyebrows have quirked and held up. Something is off. If I'm not mistaken, Simon has been speaking with an American accent.

"Please, Simon, please," Cherry begs as she dramatically thrashes her head back and forth as if she'll die of need.

My heart feels like it's stopped cold turkey when his butt cheeks clench as he lowers himself, thrusting into her so hard and fast that it seems as if he's trying to break through her. Grunting, he pumps roughly.

I close my eyes and purse my lips, keeping myself from rushing into his bedroom and pounding him with my fists. I've never felt so powerless. In my face—they're screwing right in front of me. But damn it, I can't stop them. I need money. I need Simon one hundred percent in my corner during negotiations with Jaycee. *Damn it.* This is why I hate Hollywood. That cheating bastard that I said I'd marry stands between me and the cash I need to keep my restaurant alive.

"Oh yeah, baby," he repeats in what I'm certain is an American accent.

Does he fake his English accent? And if so, then Cherry must know the truth, because she doesn't seem surprised by it.

I take a swift step back and paste myself against the wall. I feel so stuck between a rock and a hard place, and the frustration of it, the power-lessness of it, makes me want to cry. But I don't want to cry over the mockery Simon's made of our relationship. He hasn't broken my heart, but my ego is definitely bruised.

What the hell, I mouth as I squeeze my temples. I have to get out of this godforsaken trailer. The heated air feels like it's choking me. And with every thrust into Cherry Atwell's eager vag, bile rises from my stomach into my throat, forcing me to swallow to keep from throwing up.

I'm shaking all over, but my steps stay quiet as

I tiptoe away from the offensive act, clutching my stomach again. I feel even sicker realizing that I'll have to come back later and pretend as if I haven't seen them together. However, after I persuade him to stand behind me as I hammer out a new deal with Jaycee, the shit will roll downhill and bury him alive. That, I promise.

I release one shaky breath as I carefully open the door.

"There she is!" Brandi, one of the likable PAs, says way too loudly. She's never looked so wired, and it takes me a moment to fully focus and comprehend the reality of why.

My jaw drops further. I'm aware that my feet should step over the threshold of Simon's trailer. I should get out of the doorway. Otherwise, I risk them hearing us. But I can't move an inch.

"Dad?" My tight, dry throat is barely able to choke out the word.

Even though tears stream from my eyes, I can see that my dad looks like the billions he's worth in his expensive slacks, Italian leather shoes, and a black cashmere trench coat. Everything and everyone out here is covered in mud, grass, and pollen, but not him. He's impeccable.

He looks as if he's about to say something

until his eyebrows pull up and his glare rises above my head to stare daggers at something behind me.

"Treasure? Doll? Did you knock?" Simon says using his English accent. His tone is lazy, like he's trying to deceive me into believing that he's been asleep and not banging Cherry Attwell.

Tears produced by sheer anger blur my vision as I turn to face Simon. He's a few feet behind me, standing as if he's trying to guard the hallway.

"What's going on out there?" Cherry asks, appearing beside him, wrapped in nothing but a white sheet. Her barely visible feline smile is made just for me.

Simon and I lock eyes. I'm reading something in them that I can't quite figure out.

"Um, well, okay," Brandi says as if she's found herself in a situation to which there is no real proper response to.

Simon grumbles something indecipherable to Cherry, who immediately scurries away.

He puts a hand on my shoulder, but I rip myself from his touch and rush down the short set of stairs.

My feet thump down the boardwalk and arrive in front of my dad, who is an immovable object. His familiar scent drifts over me, filling my eyes with more tears that I fight like hell to contain. And Leo hasn't said anything yet. He's just checking out the scene, for sure judging.

I hear Simon's trailer door close. He must've cowered in the face of my dad's hawkish glower. I'm satisfied that my dad has intimidated him. But all I can do is clench my back teeth to keep my chin from quivering. I can't even ask my dad the obvious question, which is, what is he doing here. Because if I do…

Don't cry, Treasure.

Don't you even think about it.

Then, without saying anything at all, my dad wraps his arms around me, and for several seconds, being this close to his subtle and familiar apple-mint-vanilla-sandalwood scent makes me feel safe, secure, and—even though we haven't been very close since he cut me off from the family's money ten years ago—truly loved. So I release my tears with a shoulder-jerking, wet-face kind of ugly cry, knowing my dad just might make it all better.

What's the Deal

TREASURE GROVE

Thankfully, my tiny trailer is mildly clean. I don't think my dad cares how large my space is, but still, I want him to see that a small part of me has her shit together, and that is not what's on display in this crappy trailer.

"You can sit here," I say, pulling out one of two hard black plastic chairs, which are partnered with a rickety card table. I spot my unmade bed and resist the urge to groan about not making it. I barely made it out of here and to the set on time this morning.

My dad tilts his chin as if regarding me with concern as he lowers himself into the chair. He seems so tense and nervous as his probing eyes take in the space.

Feeling his gaze sink through me, I fold my arms tighter against my chest, thinking maybe I understand why he's looking at me that way. "I know the trailer is small. It's just, I'm rarely in this thing. Just to sleep. I'm mostly on set." I frame my lips into the fakest smile on earth, hiding the fact that this trailer and being on set make me feel as if I'm dying on the inside.

"This is fine," he says as he rolls his shoulders back to sit taller. But if it's so fine, then why does he look so uneasy?

Suddenly, it dawns on me that something could be very wrong. Swallowing a gasp, I press my hand snuggly over my heart to ask, "Is Mom okay?"

Leo's palm flies up. "Your mom is perfect."

"Okay then." My tone connotes that I'm seeking an explanation as to why he's in Iceland, which happens to be an ocean away from where he lives.

His mouth twitches as he presses his lips. He's definitely nervous. I would ask if Lynx is still in good health, but then, I would know if anything bad has happened to Lynx before he would. I'm Lynx's emergency contact. I'm not even sure he and our dad are on speaking terms.

With a sigh, Leo seems to relax a bit. Then he rubs his palms against his pants as his eyebrows bounce up and down. He's acting exactly like he did before he told me he was cutting me off from the family riches.

"I guess you want to know why I'm here," he says.

My chest tightens, and I nod stiffly. "Yeah. Why are you here?" Somehow, the volume of my voice feels inadequate, or maybe, I feel inadequate.

My dad crosses his leg like he does when he's about to talk business. *So he's here for business, and his visit isn't personal.* That's almost a relief. "I have a proposition for you," he says.

I stand tall without uncrossing my arms. "Okay…" I say, sounding guarded.

"You know the Lord family, don't you?"

The Lords? He means the family that's been nothing but an enemy to our family ever since I could remember. However, as recently as five days ago, the bad blood may have been purged when my cousin Paisley became engaged to Hercules, the youngest Lord brother. And we both know that I had a fling with Orion once—well, twice—but Leo only knows about the one.

However, the plot has definitely thickened. Like a shark smells blood in the water, I smell money in the air. But I keep a straight face. I don't want my dad to know that my interest has been highly piqued.

"Mm-hmm," I say tightly then swallow.

My dad makes a sudden move to take off his coat, leaving me wondering why in the hell he's tiptoeing around whatever he's here to say, which is totally out of character for him. Something has to be very wrong.

My arms fall to my side as my heart constricts, and I say, "Dad. Is everything okay with you?" Maybe he's here to tell me has cancer or something. He would totally do that.

"I'm fine," he says, frowning as if his demise is the last thing I should suspect.

"Okay then…" It's time he gets on with it. The suspense is driving me crazy on the inside, so much so, that it feels like Simon's infraction never even happened.

Leo coolly lays his expensive coat over his lap. "I heard about what happened to you on set this morning."

I stiffen, wondering who told him. Was it

Brandi? She can be a motormouth when she's nervous. My dad makes everybody nervous.

"If you're putting yourself through this because you need money, then I might have a solution," he says, recrossing his legs.

I'm listening attentively as he goes on about bank regulations and interest paid on holdings. It's all high, apparently. Operating the family bank, Grove Industrial Tech, and several other businesses as separate entities and treating them as such has been a nightmare. He mentions old-money sweetheart deals. Apparently, the Lords have some unique wealth maintenance privileges. My ears perk up higher when he says that Paisley's engagement to Hercules Lord has put our family in a position to be granted entrance into what he calls "the land that flows with milk and honey."

I actually snicker at that. My dad smiles as if he enjoys lightening my mood. He actually used to make me laugh a lot before he dropped the bomb on me. We were close. I'm still baffled at why he so abruptly cut me off.

He continues, mentioning the upcoming marriage between Paisley and Hercules, and he does so without grimacing. *Interesting.*

21

"The assets between Xan and me are split fifty-fifty, and then we are executors of our children's trusts."

I fidget nervously as I keep myself from screaming, "Why?" at the top of my lungs. *Why in the hell do you keep me from what Grandfather made rightfully mine?* All I want is my restaurant. Just a tiny bit of my inherited money will help me keep it alive. Given another opportunity, I will not make the same operational mistakes twice.

My dad pauses to get a read on me. But I'm totally confused about why I should care about the family's banking concerns, especially when I've been separated from the money.

He coughs to clear his throat and then shimmies his back against the flimsy chair, which creaks. I'm embarrassed again. But he's nervous. "However, if another Grove marries into the Lord family, then we will qualify for those inherited entitlements."

A lot of questions and few expletives are sprinting across my brain. Leo watches me as if he knows he has to give me time to think. In actuality, he hasn't really asked me to do anything yet, but I think I know what he wants me to do.

Shit.

As I blink, my eyes get stuck closed for a few seconds. There's no way this is really happening. Except it certainly is.

"You want me to marry one of the Lord brothers?" A humorless laugh escapes me. It's just so ridiculous and surreal.

My dad's thick eyebrows quirk up, and I know the answer to my question.

"Am I being punked?" I ask for purposes of clarification, although I've never known Leo Grove to be a prankster.

Leo looks confused. "Punked? What's that?"

Okay… so I'm not being punked. I barely shake my head. "It's a TV show."

My dad shakes his head, grimacing. "Then, no, you're not being punked."

My lips form an O and remain stuck in that shape. When I find my muscles and voice again, I say, "Then you're serious."

Wearing a sober frown, my dad nods sharply.

Holy shit. The craziness of what he's asking makes me laugh. I picture the Lord brothers. I faintly recall what Achilles looks like. But Orion's face pops up vividly as I recall how he dry humped my ass in public last Friday. Gross. After what he did to me, simply gross. Then there is

Body overheating, I tug at the collar of my fur dress. I had forgotten that I was still wearing this ridiculous costume. I want to rip it off, but I also want to scream at my dad. I mean… is that how much of my money he's been keeping from me? I've been struggling to make ends meet, doing whatever it takes. And I'm not rich girl whining either. I put every single dime I had left into my restaurant. But all this time, the money I needed has been sitting in a bank account, and I couldn't have it just because my dad said no.

Suddenly, my head feels like it's lodged between the tongs of a nutcracker. I squeeze my temples to relieve the tightness. "I can't believe you," I blurt. I didn't mean to say that out loud.

"I figured you might feel that I have no right to ask for your help."

I jerk my had back as I scoff. "We're calling it 'help'? No, you're not helping me, Dad. You're helping yourself. And you've been holding my money for all these years. All of that money!" Fingers stiff, I'm throttling my hands in frustration. I can't believe him.

"Treasure Chest, I did it for your own good. And look at you"—he gives this cruddy trailer a once-over—"you're thriving."

My laugh is dark. "What?" I continue laughing because what he said was pure comedy. "You call this thriving?" I throw my hands up wildly, inviting him to get a good look at how I'm living. "I can't act my way out of a paper bag, Dad. I've been trying though and making a fool of myself while doing it. But I need the money."

My mouth is stuck open. What more can I say? I don't want to full-on complain about being broke. In actuality, I survived pretty okay until I bought the restaurant. And I love my restaurant even if it's breaking me faster than a speeding bullet. Pretty soon, I won't have a dime to my name.

He's nodding as if he understands why I'm so overcharged. "Do you remember the Bessers?"

The Bessers? Who the hell are they? And why is he asking me about them? No one comes to mind, so I swiftly shake my head, agitated.

"Bryce Besser's grandfather was one of our early investors. You met Bryce and his three daughters. But you were probably too young to remember them." Knitting his eyebrows together thoughtfully, my dad raises a finger. "One of the girls broke something of yours. It made you cry."

Now I remember. "Oh yes." Three very scary

little faces populate my memory. Even though I can't fully recall what they looked like, I can recall every bit of how they made me feel. "Those girls," I say as if I'm barfing the words. "They were awful. They broke the jewelry box Grandma gave me."

My dad nods as if he's recalling how I cried to my mom, who held me. She took me out for ice cream and a movie to help me feel better. When we returned home later that evening, much to my relief, the girls were gone.

My dad says that Bryce Besser died in March of the same year he stopped my trust payments. The daughters, who had nothing going for themselves, never knew that Bryce had lost all the family wealth. He'd been living on an over-bloated stipend handed to him by his father's company's board of directors. The board had taken pity on Bryce and paid him a heavy monthly salary, which was enough to keep up his lifestyle. After the father passed, the stipend stopped. His daughters and wife were left with hardly anything to live on.

"Those girls had no survival instincts to make it on their own. Sweetheart, I felt you were heading down that same path. We'd given you too much. Your mom had to be convinced, but she eventually said she trusted me. But look at you," he says, holding up his hands like he's presenting me to the world. "You've been tried and tested. You're doing what needs to be done to get what you want out of life. I see that you hate being here. But you're here, doing what needs to be done to ensure your success. I'm proud of you, Treasure Chest—very proud of you."

"Don't take any credit for me." My words come out sharper than a razor's edge.

I'm glaring at my dad, and he's watching with a receptive expression. But still, I can tell that he feels no remorse for his decision.

Finally, elbows out to his sides, he smashes his palms against his thighs and sets his penetrating glare on me. "Treasure Island—remember that place?" His eyebrows quirk up. "Huh?"

My face tightens, and so does my mouth as I nod.

"But first, you went on that reality show where you spent money so fast to show off a lifestyle we never approved of. The expenses you racked up went way beyond your inheritance payments. Xan was filtering in extra money to your account. I couldn't keep up with how much you were spending. Then you didn't finish college. For goodness' sake, who quits Smith College with a respectable 3.6 GPA?"

My dad sighs forcefully as he massages his temples now. He's worked himself into a frenzy as he went from composed to exorbitantly gesticulating with his hands. And frankly, I never saw myself through his eyes until after hearing everything he said—all of my major fuckups, sans the restaurant, laid bare before me.

My throat is tight, but I manage to eke out, "I'm sorry." I can't believe I said that, but I meant it.

Leo drops his hands from his forehead and looks at me as if he can't believe I apologized either.

I shrug. "You're right. I used to go through a lot of money. But look at me now." I look down at myself in the ugly costume I'm wearing. "I received your message loud and clear."

My dad studies my wry smile and then chuckles a sigh.

"Listen, I know what I'm asking you to do is unorthodox," he says in a tender and convincing voice. "And I might be crossing a line here that

I'm not quite comfortable with. But since you've had a relationship with one the Lord brothers…"

"No!" I shout, shaking my head vigorously. "Never will I ever marry Orion Lord. No." I set my chin and purse my lips defiantly. Because I mean it.

"Okay." Leo's tone is cautious and uncertain. "Well, you don't have to live with him. It'll all only be on paper."

"That's not how Orion operates," I say, still shaking my head. But hell if I'm going to let one hundred fifty-three million dollars slip through my fingers. "I'll marry Achilles—on paper. And only Achilles." Because Achilles is like a sleek and independent cat that will go somewhere and hide unless he wants something that's very, very, very important, and it won't be sex. I've heard in circles that Orion and I share that Achilles is either not into women or is a sort of self-ordained monk, vowing celibacy, chastity, and obedience to his family—but poverty? Never.

Our Meeting Is Not Cute

TREASURE GROVE

S ix hours later, I sit in the back seat of the Grove family chauffeured car, staring into the lobby of the Grove Family Bank Tower past sparkling-clean glass windows. My flight landed in Teterboro less than an hour ago. It felt like forever since I'd flown on a Grove family private jet. My dad couldn't travel with me. He flew onward to London to handle Grove Industrial Tech, better known as GIT, business. I'm relieved that we parted ways. I wouldn't know what to say to him during a five-hour flight to the city. I'm happy he explained why he cut me off in the first place, but still, he should've told me about the Besser daughters from the start. Maybe I would've chosen to stop spending frivolously on

my own. I picture myself back then. To be fair...
nah, I wouldn't have made that choice back then.

On the flight over the Atlantic Ocean, I constantly worried about the deal going south before the wheels of the airplane touched ground. But I made it to my final destination, and as far as I'm aware, the deal is still on. I can already feel the money gracing my fingertips.

The driver opens my door, and when I have two feet on the sidewalk, he says, "I'll be waiting for you, Miss Grove."

Before I can say there's no need to wait, my attention is hijacked by a tall, strapping man wearing an impeccable suit. For some reason, I can't look away from him. His gait resembles that of someone who descends from royalty. And it's not his neatly trimmed five-o'clock shadow, perfectly formed forehead, sharp cheekbones, and kissable lips that steal my attention either—it's his confidence that demands to be noticed.

As if sensing me staring, the man stops and turns. I suspend breathing when our eyes meet. His face looks... oh my God. I gasp a quick breath of air. The man is Achilles Lord. It's been ages since I've seen him in the flesh.

I absentmindedly fan my fingers over my

collarbone with one hand and wave tentatively at him with the other. Instead of waving back, he frowns, leaving me feeling stupefied and confused. Why is he staring at me with such a severe scowl? He looks as if I've just kicked him in the shin or something.

This morning, my dad stepped out of my trailer to negotiate the details of our marriage contract with Achilles. By the gestures he was making, I could tell that my insistence to marry him instead of Orion hadn't gone down easy. Maybe he's mad that I refuse to marry his brother. I'm certain he doesn't know why I'm so insistent about keeping my distance from Orion. His brother would never tell him what he did in St. Barts. That incident was the straw that broke the camel's back as far as I was concerned.

Even though being given the cold shoulder by Achilles stings a little, I will not change my mind, not at this juncture. And frankly, Achilles should be happy that he's marrying me. I don't want to infringe on whatever or whomever he does during his free time. There are plenty of rumors about him floating around. I've learned that rumors aren't always true, but still, I want to assure him that he doesn't have to worry about my wanting more than a nonexistent relationship.

I flash him a final smile to convince him that his assholish glower hasn't deterred me, but his frown turns worse. Then he stiffens as if he's just realized the error of his response to me, rips his eyes away from my face, and continues to stride a little less confidently into the building.

"Miss Grove, is everything okay?" the driver asks.

"Yes," I say, blinking myself back into the moment. Shaking like a leaf in the wind, I tell the driver that his services will not be needed. But still, I can't get what just happened between Achilles and me out of my head. This arrangement of ours might be harder than I thought.

ACHILLES STANDS IN FRONT OF THE SEMICIRCLE-shaped reception desk that has platinum siding and a white quartzite top. The three women working behind the barrier behold his amazingly handsome face as though it's a never-before-seen masterpiece by Chagall. For a moment, I feel as if time has stalled and I'm able to take in the entire scene without being noticed. For instance, each receptionist wears the same kind of smart black suit with a crisp white blouse buttoned to the neck. Each has her hair pulled back into a tight bun that clings to the nape of her neck, so it's easy to see that all their faces have turned various shades of red, depending on the hue of their skin. They only turn to acknowledge me when Achilles does. His disapproving gaze runs up and down my body. Looking into that gaze reminds me that I'm wearing faded bell-bottom blue jeans with a fitted, crisp white button-front blouse that has oversized sleeves. My hair billows from a loose topknot. And since the weather is warmer and more humid in New York than Iceland, as soon as I deplaned, I rummaged through my suitcase and found my gladiator sandals. I look down at my feet and then at Achilles. It's apparent that he's judging me for being the only underdressed person in the room. I probably should've worn something else, but I did the best I could with what I had, being that I didn't pack any business-formal attire to take with me to Iceland. So screw Achilles. He doesn't get to judge me anyway. *What an asshole.*

Shoulders back, I finish closing the distance between me and the desk.

"Hi, I'm Treasure Grove," I say, pretending Achilles is not with us, although his cologne smells searingly delicious. My nostrils detect hints of sandalwood, apple, and black pepper. I can feel him looking at me still. *What's his deal?* I never back down from a passive-aggressive challenge, but I'm feeling myself shrink under his glare. I hate that I'm responding to him this way. I should purse my lips and dress him down properly, but I can't do it. He's won. I'm intimidated by him.

"Yes, Miss Grove. We've been expecting you," the girl whose name tag says Tonia remarks before shifting her dutifully friendly eyes to Achilles. "Will you both follow me?"

Achilles waits for me to walk first. I continue to avoid eye contact with him as I follow the receptionist through a white-walled corridor with clean gray sandstone floors. It's been a long time since I've walked this path, but I know it well. We're on our way to the secure elevators that go directly to my uncle Xander's office.

Gosh, he's walking so close behind me. Thankfully, the clacking of Tonia's heels and Achilles's dress shoes echoes loudly enough to make it impossible for any awkward attempts at small talk. But why does my head feel so cloudy?

Why am I able to sense his every movement? The subtle power of that cologne he's wearing continues to wash over me. Orange blossom—I missed that scent at first, but it's plainly there. I would compliment him on the scent if he weren't behaving like a storm cloud. I figure if Achilles is pretending that I don't exist, then I should do the same. He's already setting the tone for our affiliation, and heck, I think I like it.

"Tonia," I say now that my inner dialogue has made me feel a lot more relaxed.

Tonia raises her eyebrows up high as we stop at the platinum-plated elevators. "Yes, Miss Grove." Her smile and voice are less robotic. I think it's because I referred to her by her name.

"Is my mom, Londyn Grove, around?" She runs the Grove Philanthropic Foundation and has an office in the building and on the same floor as my uncle Xander. I would love to stop by and see her. I hadn't laid eyes on her since Christmas Day dinner.

"No, Londyn, I mean, Mrs. Grove is uptown on business," she says, pressing her finger to the identification pad.

Grunting, I feel a stab of disappointment. I would've loved to hug and kiss her. I've been missing her and too preoccupied with my own life and worries to make a plan to meet her for brunch. "Oh well, thanks for letting me know."

The elevators begin to slide open. "But I can let her know you inquired about her."

"That'd be nice."

Her smile takes a different dimension as the doors finish sliding open. "By the way, I really love the food at TCC."

I hesitate before slapping a hand over my chest. Is that what people are calling my fine five-star dining restaurant, TCC? That sounds like a chain-food restaurant or a yogurt shop. I'll have to change the name of my restaurant after the renovation. But this deal isn't set in stone yet. Anything can happen, especially since Achilles is behaving like sour candy.

"Really?" I say in a high-pitched voice, forcing myself back to the moment.

"Very much so, and we'll be back soon."

"Then…" I look over at Achilles, who surprisingly appears to be patiently watching the exchange between me and Tonia. I thought he'd be tapping his watch, signaling that he has more important things to do than listen to two girls prattle on about a restaurant he'll never visit.

Regardless, I don't want to be rude, so I step into the elevator and then turn around to ask her, "What's your last name?"

She appears surprised, like she knows she's about to receive a reward. "Um, Gamble."

"Tonia Gamble," I say as I move over and give space for Achilles to enter. "I'll put you on the guest list. Anytime you want a reservation, we'll find space for you. And your next five dinners are on us." I raise a finger as the doors begin to close. "That includes you and your guests."

Tonia belts a loud and happy "thank you" before I'm shut into the elevator alone with Achilles.

"You'll never make money giving away dinners for free."

I startle in surprise. It almost sounds like his voice whispered from the heavens. "Ah," I say, quirking an eyebrow with intrigue. "So he does speak."

His serious grimace is pinned to my face. We're just staring at each other as the elevator soars to the top floor. The silence between us is torturous and awkward. But the ball is in his court. He's supposed to respond to my last comment with something. Anything. But he doesn't. The thing is, I haven't gotten this far in life by playing asshole with an asshole. So I reach inside myself for genuine empathy for this dick and release a sharp sigh before finding the best smile I can muster.

"How was your morning, Mr. Lord?" I ask in a syrupy voice.

I'm waiting for something on his face to change, but his pressed lips and the puckered skin between his eyebrows don't ease up. But still, I wait expectantly for him to say something anyway. Goodness gracious, he can't be this socially awful.

"It was fine," he replies quietly.

Pressing my fingers to my collarbone, I lean toward him like I have a secret to tell him. "I know this is awkward. But believe me, whatever you do, whoever you are, will not be exposed by me."

His eyes contract even more as his glare laps my face. It's like he didn't hear a thing I just said. Then he leans away from me. "You look different."

I tip my head to one side. I didn't expect him to say that. "Of course I look different. You haven't seen me since I was a kid. I'm a woman now." My smile is friendly. I want him to recognize that I'm lightening the mood, showering sunshine over his storm cloud.

But Achilles's expression doesn't wane. "Right, right…" he whispers thoughtfully.

The way he continues staring at me has rendered me speechless. Is that attraction I see in his eyes? If so, then why the frown? Gosh, he's so hard to read. But tingles of sensation fluttering through my heart and lady parts scare me. Especially when in one flashing moment, I admit to myself that I would fuck him. I seriously would. He smells divine. He has the sort of looks that make men envy him and women crave him. And his body… he's a bona fide Adonis. I can visualize the ripple of his abs and see them pushing against the fabric of his suit jacket.

The thought makes me swallow a gasp and stare at the floor.

No, I can't. I just can't.

"Are you…" he starts but the doors slide open.

The welcome sight of my uncle Xander fills the frame and steals both of our attention.

"Treasure Chest," Xander says, unfolding his arms from his chest and holding them out to receive me.

"Xan," I sing and then kiss him on the cheek, and then we give each other a heartfelt hug. I haven't seen my uncle since Christmas either. But I love that he's always so happy to see me. He smells a lot like Achilles and my dad—it's a rich man's scent.

Xan leans back to get a look at me, and his smile is tight. His eyes jump around my face as if he's trying to get a read on how I feel about signing away my freedom.

"You okay with this?" he asks.

"I am," I say, reassuring him with a smile. I really am okay with it, but I just want this part to be over already.

He nods stiffly and then looks up at my future husband. "Good afternoon, Achilles." Just like his expression, Xan's voice is all business.

"Good afternoon, Xander." All business there too.

Apparently, cutting a deal together doesn't mean the Groves and Lords will automatically become best buddies. I recall how much Achilles and my cousin Max, who is co-CEO of GIT along with my dad, hate each other. It wouldn't be a stretch to believe that Xan, who normally doesn't have a hateful bone in his body, would dislike Achilles in support of his only son.

Achilles impatiently checks his watch. "We should get this over with. I have meetings."

Xan's left eyebrow quirks up as if he's curious to know about the meetings Achilles is referring to. Then Xan asks me to lead the way. As the two men walk behind me, they quickly engage in a spirited back-and-forth about Achilles's cousin Nero. Xan wants to know the point of the documents that Nero had sent over late yesterday afternoon.

"Ask him," Achilles says in dismissive tone as we enter Xan's main office.

"Why can't you let TRANSPOT go? It was just a pipe dream my father had," Xan replies.

"If it's just a pipe dream, then give us what we want, and it all stops."

I can't see them because I'm taking in an eyeful of the better part of Xan's large office. But I can feel them glaring at each other. Our families have been fighting over TRANSPOT since forever. It's some sort of technological possibility, the merging of computer technology and astrophysics. That's how my grandfather explained it. Basically, that relationship will create software that's able to make 3-D image projections into solid figures. It's a complicated invention, at least to me it is. My cousin Paisley, Xan's only daughter, a beautiful nerd, has been working on the software since high school. I think she's actually getting close to making it happen. I'm indifferent about it all. I'm not a computer person. I'm a restaurant owner, which is why I'm here saving my restaurant.

But I had forgotten how breathtaking Xan's office is. First of all, he has stellar views of the Hudson to the south and the rest of Manhattan to the east and north. The solid furniture like his desk, the long conference table, end tables, and large block coffee table are made of the finest light beechwood. The sturdy furniture is uphol-stered with gray tweed fabric which he pairs with bold pops of modernity like colorful abstracts and contemporary bar lamps on the walls and arcing floor lamps positioned throughout. Combined with the breathtaking views, Xan's office is the perfect place to hang out all day and get a lot of work done. I think I'm going to follow his design lead when I finally have my money and start reno-vations on my restaurant. The changes will happen fast, starting today.

"Let's sit," Xan says, lowering himself into one of the large armchairs facing a long sofa.

I thought Achilles would take the chair adjacent Xan's. That's what my dad would do. He calls it "never losing the advantage." The man in the big chair has the power. But instead of matching Xan pound for pound, Achilles sits next to me on the sofa, and rather close too.

I work to keep my breaths even as Xan says that since I've been engaged to Simon for three months, it will sound more believable if the marriage between Achilles and me is announced early September.

Achilles's sharp grunt signals he disapproves. "No. The sooner the better."

Smirking wryly, Xan asks, "Why the rush?"

Achilles leans forward. "Why are you dragging this out? That's not the deal."

Oh gosh, my head feels light. I try very hard to maintain my patience. Part of me wants to run away from this situation as fast as I can. I want to get this over with. And I don't want Achilles and Xan to blow up this deal.

"Can we just get this over with?" I blurt. "No one who knows Simon or I expected us to actually go through with it anyway. Plus, he's a cheater. He cheated on me. *TRM* has already posted about it, and now everybody knows."

Silence sticks in the air. I don't look up to see the pity on their faces. I'm the one who chose to become involved with a cad like Simon Linney. He's not the kind of guy a girl gets involved with if she's expecting a solid happily ever after.

"I'm sorry to hear that, Treasure Chest," Xan finally says.

"Four weeks," Achilles cuts in behind him.

I allow myself to look at my in-name-only future husband. There's not a sign of sympathy on his face. Achilles is all business.

"That's one month," Xan says, rubbing his chin thoughtfully.

Achilles tilts his head in my direction without looking at me. "That will give her the appropriate number of days to grieve."

"I'm not grieving over Simon," I say past my tight throat.

We're staring into each other's eyes, and my breaths feel craggy until I let my gaze fall to my lap. *Why does he make me feel this way?*

"All right then, four weeks." Xan rubs his palms together. "Let's get the show on the road."

"Wait," I say, holding my hand up. I've been

wanting to know something since I accepted to go through with this charade. I face Achilles. "What do you get out of this?"

"That's none of your concern," Achilles retorts in what seems to be his normal hissing voice.

Wow. He really doesn't like me. Actually, his tone stings a little. But I dare not show it.

"Why not?" I ask, refusing to back down. "I'll be your wife. So what's yours will be mine and vice versa." I smirk because I'm screwing with him. He's such an asshole, why not have some fun with it?

He snorts bitterly and then readjusts in his seat. "Our benefit has to do with the Lord family trust."

The fact that he answered my question renders me speechless for moment. I turn my surprised expression away from Achilles Lords's spectacular face to look at Xan. "All right, then," I say, sounding winded. With one quick cough, I clear my throat. "We should continue. I have a lot to do today too."

"Like what?" Achilles blurts.

I'm not the only one who's looking at Achilles with surprise. Nobody expected him to ask me that.

It appears as if he's trying to mask his own shock as well. His question was definitely a slip of the tongue.

"Like, a lot," I say, folding my arms on my chest defiantly.

"Just be careful," Achilles warns.

"Wow," I let out with a harsh laugh. "You really don't like me, do you?"

Again, he frowns at me as though I'm the sole reason for his crappy life. *What in the hell does that look mean?* "I don't know you, Miss Grove. Therefore, I cannot dislike you."

My lips won't move. But my brain shouts, *You asshole. He doesn't know me?* I want to mention how he ranted and raved like a lunatic after catching me and Orion together years ago. We were just teenagers. He could have been less of an asshole about it. "And by the way, never have I ever been or will I ever be a debutante," I say, remembering he called me that way back when.

We suddenly become engaged in an epic staring battle. I refuse to be the first to look away.

Xan claps his hands loudly enough that we mutually break eye contact. "Let's focus," my uncle says. But I know Xan very well. He's studying us both, wondering what in the hell just happened. And it's evident that he doesn't like our exchange at all, not in the least.

FINALLY, IT'S TIME. I'M SO CLOSE TO THE MONEY, I can taste it. A lawyer brings in the contracts. His name is Clive. He's young and handsome and he never fails to look at me with flirtatious eyes. Halfway through the ritual of handing the pen to Achilles so that he can sign and date and then hand it back to me, I remember that Clive is the lawyer who went on a date with Paisley. At least I now understand why he's so flirtatious. Paisley and I resemble each other. He probably sees me as a second shot at her, but that will never happen. Despite the obvious—I'm signing a contract to marry another man—Paisley and I never date each other's exes, and that includes guys who were once interested in one of us.

The stack of documents to sign seems to go on forever as Clive explains the significance of each. I think the exercise feels so arduous because Achilles is too close. His body heat warming my backside is having a dizzying effect on me. There's no way in the world Achilles Lord should be making me feel this way.

Then, our fingers brush during a transfer of the pen. Giddy energy rises up my arm, captures my heart, and takes a nosedive down to my core. However, I play it off as if I feel nothing. But Achilles must've felt it too, because his fixed grimace intensifies as he asks Xander for his own "writing instrument."

What the fuck?

Who calls a pen a "writing instrument," anyway? Nope. I'm done with jerks, and he's a jerk. I'd rather screw the happy-go-lucky and super-nice Ronald McDonald than Achilles Lord. Keeping that in mind, I put a mental wall between him and me, knowing that although we'll be married in four weeks, I will not have to see or talk to him for the duration of our nuptials. Then I'll divorce him, and we'll never have to think about each other ever again. *What a prick!*

Breaking the News

ACHILLES LORD

I pace my office floor like a caged bull. Rarely do I let my nerves get the better of me. It's been three days since I've seen Treasure Grove. I don't remember her being so drop-dead gorgeous. I stop to touch my eyebrow as I squeeze my eyes shut. *Damn.* She's not even my type. She strikes me as irresponsible and flighty. Who in the hell shows up to sign important documents wearing faded blue jeans? Bell-bottoms? Is this the seventies? That was unprofessional of her.

But the way her jeans cradled her ass…

The mounds of honey-brown hair pinned loosely on the top of her head, drawing attention to her pretty heart-

shaped face… I didn't know she had a smattering of freckles across her nose. It's cute. She's cute. And her lips…

"Shit."

I flex my fingers as if grabbing at the air. I don't like being anxious, and thinking about her makes me anxious. I've been wishing I would've made Orion step up to the plate and do something for the family for once. I could've ridden his ass all the way to the finish line. But it's too late to back out now. I'll have to keep my distance from Treasure Grove. I have no doubt she will stay far away from me.

Why did she give me so much attitude anyway?

And I called her a debutante?

I don't remember that. "Debutante" isn't even in my vocabulary. When I found her and Orion in bed together in the manor on our grandfather's private island in Nova Scotia, admittedly, I was incensed. But my anger was directed at my brother, not her. She was the injured party, caught up in Orion's dark allure.

"Shit." I did call her a debutante. I rub the back of my neck. "She remembers that?"

Finally, Orion blows into my office as if he doesn't have a care in the world. "Remember what?" He plops down on my sofa, spreading his arm across the top, legs wide, slouching.

Glowering at him, I take full responsibility for his blasé attitude. I, and a host of other enablers, have been picking up his slack for far too long.

"You're twenty-three minutes late," I grumble.

He spreads his legs wider and humps the air with his crotch. "I had business to take care of. I'll be a married man soon. So I had to sew some wild oats."

His grin is salacious. No wonder Treasure Grove doesn't want anything to do with him. I don't know her that well, but judging from the way she carries herself, she's too good for him.

I slap the top of my desk and snap, "Sit the fuck up." I wanted to take a more sympathetic approach with him, but he's making that impossible

He slowly gives me the posture I want him to have. "What the fuck, Achilles?"

I shake my head, gradually bringing my anger under control. The sight of him sitting in front of me without a care in the world while lazily waiting to hear that he's going to be given the ultimate prize annoys the hell out of me. I'm worried all the damn time. He's never worried. I carry the weight of this family on my shoulders. And he sucks us dry. But he's still my brother and I love him. That's why I've been stressing about telling him that I'm the one who's going to marry Treasure Grove. The news isn't going to go down easy.

I stretch my neck from side to side. The act fails to relieve the tension in my shoulders. It's time to get it over with.

"We heard back from Treasure Grove," I say.

His lips hike up into a smirk as he flagrantly grabs his cock. Treasure's not here to see him but I'm offended for her. "Oh, I can't wait. I'm going to be good to her, Achilles, real good to her."

I snort like an angry bull. "Why the hell are you grabbing your cock?" I want to slap some manners into him. "The way you're behaving is the reason she refuses to marry you."

Orion's eyebrows quirk up, holding for a moment before dropping way low. "What do you mean she's refusing to marry me? Who the fuck is she going to marry if not me?"

I stop biting down hard on my back teeth to say, "I'm marrying her."

He flies to his feet. "What?"

"It's because she wants nothing to do with you." I point at him like I want to poke his eye out. "And it's your fault. Look at how you walked in here, thrusting your cock in the air and shit."

Mouth agape and face suddenly drained of blood, he looks like I stole his lunch money. I'm sort of surprised by this reaction of his. They hadn't been together since they were eighteen or nineteen. Unless they got together again between then and now. That would make sense. The older and wiser Treasure got a taste of his bullshit. But I love him, and I feel sorry for him. Shit, he looks like he's about to pass out.

"Just sit back down," I say.

He slowly, carefully does as I ask.

"Maybe I can talk to her," he says. "Sometimes, I like to push her buttons. But I'll let her know I won't do that."

I'm shocked he's fighting for her. If she knew it, I wonder if she'd change her mind. But it doesn't matter any longer.

"You can't talk to her," I say tightly and then clear my throat.

"Why not?"

I sit on the edge of my desk. In my mind, I see Treasure and I signing the contract. Her standing too damn close. I wanted things from her that I've always had complete control over. My hand wanted to touch her perfectly round ass. My lips wanted to brush against the soft skin of her neck. Then there was her sweet scent. I'm probably one of a few men in the world who's able to control his cock. I tell it when to get hard. I let it get hard. As a strong-minded individual, I mastered the skill. Treasure Grove made me hard, and I couldn't control it. That spooks the hell out of me. Give me enough time away from her, and I'll forget she exists.

"The contracts have been signed and submitted," I say, short of breath. "The suitor can't be changed, or we risk sinking the deal."

Orion is watching me, reading me. I remain cool, calm, and collected under the force of his scrutiny.

"When?" he demands to know.

I circle my shoulders—shit, they're tight. "Three days ago."

He narrows an eye. "And you're just now telling me?"

I press my lips tighter. I don't owe him an explanation. He fucking does what I say—that's his explanation.

"Did you see her?" he asks, still eyeing me suspiciously.

I bite down hard on my back teeth as hostility rises in my throat. "Sure. Why do you ask?" My tone could freeze lava.

"Beautiful, isn't she?"

I don't say anything.

"She's got that quality. And yeah, fucking her was everything you imagine it could be. Because I know you imagine it, don't you?"

My eyes narrow to slits. I'm more angry because he's right.

Orion lets out a hostile laugh.

"What?" I bark.

My brother coolly rises to his feet. "Nothing. Is that all?"

I don't know—the way he's acting unsettles me. He's planning to do something stupid. He's in fight mode—the kind where you don't see him coming.

"Don't make contact with her, and you know why," I barely say.

He snorts bitterly and then walks to the doorway but stops before leaving my office. Without facing me, he says, "I never thought you and I would have something in common. But I want her. And I'm going to get her."

I pound my fist on the top of my desk. *Shit.*

My knuckles sting, but I welcome the pain. "Stay the fuck away from her," I boom. "If you fuck this up, then you're going to lose everything, because I'm going to take it all from you."

He turns, and our eyes are locked and loaded on each other. He knows I mean business. Hell, I know it too.

"I will stop every dollar of the Lord trust from entering your bank account if you ruin this opportunity for us," I say tightly.

Gradually, the hard look in his eyes diminishes and his mouth slackens. I can tell that he wants to plead his case to have Treasure Grove yet again. I actually feel sorry for him. I'm certain he doesn't love her, though. Orion is incapable of that. I often wonder where it went wrong with him— why does he insist on being a fuckup?

Regardless of how angry he's made me, I feel sorry for him. "Orion," I say, wanting to clean up this tragic moment we're having. But my voice falters, and he walks out, leaving me and the explanation I'm unable to give him behind.

Reopening Night

TREASURE GROVE

28 DAYS LATER

Tonight is a celebration. The song slithering through the air like a hypnotizing fog is Joon Neon's *I Want More*. I haven't danced all night, because I've been making sure my guests are happy and impressed by my restaurant's new face, new mood, new attitude, and new name. Instead of The Chest of Chelsea or the shortened version that I hated, TCC, it's now just *Treasures*. There's no shortening that name.

And yes, my guests are very, very, very impressed.

I've shaken hundreds of hands, given boatloads of hugs, smiled so much that my cheeks ache. I'm all out of business cards. Everybody wants to make reservations ASAP. I would say the night has been a huge success.

I inhale deeply through my nostrils, drinking it in. The smell of newness is such a potent aphrodisiac. My hazy gaze roams the expanse. My restaurant has been renovated from top to bottom. Long gone are my stabs at adding modern touches to those original art deco design elements from the Roaring Twenties. That was my way of renovating on the cheap. I could never get rid the stench of aged time, not until now— the odor is gone. Everything in my establishment is new and improved.

My interior designer Kelly and I went all-out modern contemporary while being careful not to forsake warmth and intimacy. I'm proud of the chrome circles plastered across the ceiling of this room. There are hundreds of them, each expelling subtle orange light. And encircling the dance floor are two stories of balcony seating. There's not an empty table tonight. My guests laugh, talk, drink, and some canoodle. Everyone is having a blast.

I was able to expand the square footage and add this new extension by purchasing the spaces on both sides of my business. They weren't for sale, but I offered the owners prices they couldn't refuse. This side will be used to accommodate high-end parties. The walls are soundproof to keep the noise contained. On the opposite side of the main restaurant, I added a casual cocktail lounge for more intimate gatherings. For smooth operating, I hired five times the previous number of staff, which includes a full-time accounting department and a promotions and marketing team. We all worked together to make tonight's grand reopening the success that it is.

My eyes pick out my A-list guests one by one—Ray Black, Carol Neilly, Chuck Bourne, the Nagasaki sisters, Kurt Tolle, Andrew Mates, Stella Meier... the list goes on and on. The only people missing are my cousin Paisley and her new husband and my future brother-in-law, Hercules Lord. Thinking about Paisley not being here makes my heart hurt. I could have seen her on Sunday night. Our family is having a mandatory dinner at her parents' house in Greenwich, Connecticut. But I've already made my decision—I'm not attending. I'll just pretend that I had forgotten all about it. Plus, I've been working nonstop for a month. Since this morning, I've felt it in my body. I need to rest.

Paisley would've shown up tonight, but she and Hercules are in Mumbai. She says it's business-related and swore me to secrecy, which is code for whatever she's doing in Mumbai is going to drive her brother Max crazy, crazier than he already is. I invited Max, too, but I'm not expecting him to show up. Even though my cousin annoys the hell out of me with his nitpicking and controlling ways, he is the ungettable get of the century. If he miraculously shows up, his appearance will be reported in every entertainment magazine in the country. The headline will read something like: *The hottest billionaire tech bachelor on the planet was out for a rare night on the town at his cousin's hot new restaurant.* The mention will be premium promotion and achieved for free.

Come on, Max, show up.

Aware that he has an unrequited crush on a friend of mine named Lake Clark, I added a special note at the bottom of his invitation saying that she will be in the house tonight.

Speaking of Lake, the night is nearly over, and she hasn't shown up either. The corners of my mouth pull down a bit as my heart processes her absence, too, until right on cue, I hear a familiar voice trumpet, "Treasure Chest!"

That's her.

I spin around so quickly my head dizzies. And there is my beautiful new friend, quickly closing the distance between us.

When we are in each other's embrace, we hug like our lives depend on this one moment of coming together again. I absolutely love Lake. She was Paisley's friend first, but now she's mine too. She's a natural addition to my constantly growing circle of good girlfriends.

"Your dress," she croons approvingly as we hold hands and lean back to get a good look at each other's outfits. Our tastes are oddly similar—sort of artsy chic but sexy and classy with pops of the extraordinary here and there.

"And we didn't plan this." My voice rises over the music.

I'm wearing a delicate powder-blue silk halter cocktail dress that touches my body like a sensual kiss. Lake's dress is the exact same color as mine, only hers is strapless and the bodice is made of latex and the skirt is composed of layers of tarlatan fabric. In addition, we're both wearing gold shoes! Mine are gold spiked-heel Christian

Louboutins, and hers are encrusted with gold. I'm not sure who makes them, but they look stunning.

"Great minds!" she says and apologizes for being late. She tells me that her fiancé wasn't feeling well. He was supposed to accompany her, and tonight would've been the first time he and I met. I've heard a lot about Mason, mostly that he's a good guy and Hercules Lord's best friend.

I'm on the verge of inquiring more about Mason's condition, as she looks so sad about whatever's going on with him and I wonder if it's serious, but a guy name Alex Shaw and his hot friend descend on us. I'm happy to see him even though I have a feeling Lake wanted to talk about whatever's going on with her fiancé.

Alex and I hug. His chest and arms are a solid mass of maleness, and his aftershave, body soap, and cologne are an ambrosia of deliciousness. Alex is a player for the new franchise baseball team my brother Lynx owns. We met at a party last year after the Connecticut Ramblers made the playoffs. There was a spark between us, and Lynx, who noticed us hitting it off, asked me to keep away from his players. My brother would never force me to stay away. He would only ask. And of course, I agreed. His sister dating any of his employees would be a conflict of interest.

And so I slipped out of the party without letting Alex know I was leaving. I heard he's tried to get in touch with me a few times since. He's even called the restaurant on several occasions. I've been meaning to call him back and explain why I ghosted him. But tonight, just like the first time we ever made eye contact, he looks scrumptious. And for some reason, I want to test this new background relationship I have with Achilles Lord. One night of passionate sex can be our little secret since we're not supposed to be with each other anyway.

"Congratulations," Alex croons softly in my ear. I'm still in his arms, and he's holding me for way too long.

"Thank you," I say as I pull out of his grasp. Shit. As much as I want to get it on with Alex tonight, I can't. That's why my tone is highly genial and not flirtatious at all.

His friend holds out his hand to Lake. "And I'm KJ," he says, eyebrows raised, gazing appreciatively into her eyes.

As KJ shakes her hand, Lake makes her engagement ring known.

"Engaged," KJ proclaims, letting her know that he's received her subtle message loud and clear.

"Happily," she exclaims.

Alex points at me. "But you are not engaged anymore. You're done with Linney, right?"

I roll my eyes. All night, people have been saying they're sorry to hear about how my relationship with Simon ended. "I didn't know you were *Top Rag Mag*'s demographic," I say in jest.

Alex, who has the world's most gorgeous smile, raises his hands as if to say, *You caught me.*

I'm in the middle of a laugh when arms wrap around my midsection, and a voice with an English accent says, "Hello, my love," in my ear and then pelts a tender kiss that contains a light dab of tongue on my temple.

Lake's, Alex's, and KJ's expressions are frozen in time as if they're marking the calm before the storm. I don't know what to say or do at the moment. I last heard from Simon a few days after I left Iceland. He sent me a text message, asking me to not believe what I saw with my own eyes, claiming that he and Cherry were merely running lines. He didn't know that I saw them fucking. I never told him. I'm also keeping the matter of his

68

fake accent to myself, at least for now. Simon is never to be trusted. When he wants something, he'll destroy everything in his path to get it. Unfortunately, he still wants me, and I'm not sure how he's going to take it when he finally hears of my engagement to Achilles.

Then, being the naughty boy that he is, Simon grinds me with an erection that's as hard as steel. "We miss you. So let's go somewhere quiet, you and me, and catch up."

His words sink through me like dread itself. With visions of him nailing Cherry Attwell dancing in my head, I ball up my right fist. I've never punched anyone in my life, but I really want to pound Simon one good time. But before I can decide whether to punch him or knee him in the groin, a ruckus explodes behind us. Simon's hands are off me, and the empty air cools my backside as a man shouts, "Take your hands off her!"

Lake slaps a hand over her mouth. Alex and KJ look horrified. When I turn to get the full picture of what's happening, I'm horrified too.

Top Rag Mag

A RUMBLE AT TREASURE'S GRAND REOPENING

66 Last night things got…

Well, kind of sexy, now that I think about it.

Stay with me.

Last night was the big reopening bash of Grove heiress Treasure Grove's restaurant, formerly known as The Chest of Chelsea and now called Treasures, which we at TRM agree was a smart move on her part. It was getting hard to say, honey, let's have dinner at that restaurant with the long name but bomb-ass food.

But getting back to the subject at

hand, if you weren't there, then you missed it.

Psst...

There was a brawl. On one side of the ring stood Treasure Grove's ex-fiancé and actor extraordinaire, Simon Linney, who we confirmed, if you missed it, cheated on her with none other than Cherry Attwell (refer back to our June 3rd alert).

On the other side of the ring, and shockingly so, stood Orion Lord.

Say what?

Our last report of Orion Lord and our favorite heiress together had him dry humping her in her restaurant over a month ago.

Treasure is still our favorite Grove heiress, right?

(Don't skip the poll below. Who is our favorite NYC heiress, Treasure or her super-rich and lucky cousin who managed to nab Hercules Lord, Paisley Grove?)

Now back to the deets.

Sources say Orion Lord wrestled

Simon Linney to the floor, punching him in the face while defending Treasure's honor. Apparently, the sight of two strapping men rolling around together on a hard surface was hot. It's been reported that several women, and men, orgasmed just a little.

However, we are still trying to figure out why Orion Lord attacked our favorite naughty bad-boy actor. Orion Lord does know that gorgeous face of Simon's is insured, right?

A lawsuit is sure to follow. We'll alert you when it happens. However, the question still remains—are Treasure Grove and Orion Lord a couple?

Our sources say that he's the real reason TG escaped the set of Marked by the Sword. Apparently, Mr. Lord asked her to come home to be with him, and she said, "Hell yes, you sexy thing."

The streets are talking, and they're saying that it's getting serious between the two lovebirds. Don't worry, we'll bring you every moment of their hot and heavy, or torrid, love affair.

So stay close.

TRM, bringing you the scoop before it happens.

P.S.

Don't forsake the poll! Your favorite heiress... Treasure or Paisley?

I know my choice.

The Fallout

TREASURE GROVE

I groan, rubbing one side of my aching head as I sit against the headboard. This is the third time I've read *TRM*'s alert. I should be thankful that they didn't mention the fact that I panicked and fled the scene. All I could think about was being the one responsible for ruining the contract between the Groves and Lords. We're still in the early stages of our agreement. I don't want to do anything to mess it up. Plus, during the signing process, Clive explained that if I'm found in breach of contract, then I will have to repay all the funds that have been released to me or an amount the executor of the trust sees fit—basically, the amount my dad sees fit. To be under his control sucks. But that's not the reason why I haven't spent the trust money on anything but my restaurant.

The day after I signed the contract, Xan emailed me a list of all the important parts he wanted me to examine. He circled one particular section in red ink. Apparently, I can pay the trust back any funds used before the end of the contract period, after which I'll be able to nullify the contract. And so I thought, great. I would spend as much as I needed to bedazzle my restaurant, which will surely make me a lot of money. Then, probably within two years, I'll make enough money to pay back the trust, and if I fall in love with someone else, I'll divorce Mr. Storm Cloud Achilles Lord.

As far as personal expenses go, I'm ahead of the game there too. Last Wednesday, I received a payment in the amount 330,025 dollars from Tuff Studios, the producers of *Marked by the Sword*. I emailed Jaycee to thank her. Of course, she complained about not being able to get in touch with me.

"Join the team," I said, my way of letting her know that I was unreachable on purpose.

One thing I like about Jaycee is she knows

how to get right down to business. We transitioned right into talking money. She still wants to pay me three million for my followers.

"Six," I said.

"Four," she countered.

"Five and half or nothing."

"Five."

"No."

"Five and a quarter," she shot back.

"Pay me half now and half when I deliver, and you have a deal," I said.

She took that deal. I've been using that money to pay for my personal expenses.

Shaking my head, as I once again feel the anguish of last night grip me, I cringe as I lift the bedcovers and look down at myself. I'm still wearing the dress from last night. My escape comes back to me in rapid and vivid succession. My breaths are quick as I'm surrounded by darkness in the alley. My feet burn with every pounding step because wearing those Louboutins with a certain degree of comfort had long expired. I fought back tears when I made it to the building that houses the Airbnb I've been living in for over a month.

That was so insane. As I ran, it was as though

I was having an out-of-body experience. Hands over my face, I groan into my palms. I am so embarrassed.

Then my doorbell rings, and I heave a sigh so heavy it makes me realize I'm out of breath.

"Damn it," I whisper.

It has to be my dad, or worse—it could be Max.

THE DOORBELL RINGS AGAIN.

Grabbing the knob, I crane my neck forward to look through the peephole.

"Shit."

It's not Max. Up until this very moment, I thought seeing him would be worse, but now, seeing my dad suddenly feels like the worst thing ever.

I clutch my stomach, which feels as if a boulder sits inside it. There's no use in delaying the inevitable. My face is numb as I turn the knob and blink at the eyes of my father.

The corners of Leo's mouth are pulled downward into the most awful frown.

"Good morning," I sing in a voice of manufactured cheer. Shamelessly, my goal is to affect his mood. But it doesn't work—his stern expression remains resilient.

"You're going to live with Achilles Lord. A car is waiting for you downstairs. Pete will take you to Achilles's apartment."

I gape at him as if he's lost his mind. "What? I just can't pick up and move in with Achilles. I need my…"

"You need your belongings," he says.

"Yeah," I whisper. I feel like my brain is processing what he just said way too slowly.

"Martha and Lena packed your clothing and other personal items to be transported over to Achilles's apartment. Martha knows you very well, so there shouldn't be a problem."

A sardonic laugh escapes me. "She touched my things, Dad?" Because it's funny. It's so fucking hilarious to find myself back in the same position I hated ten years ago with my dad calling the shots.

"I know," he says empathetically, to my surprise.

I jerk my head back. "You do?"

I'm sure he's about to say something else until one of his eyes narrows, and his gaze drops down to what I have on.

Dang it. Leo is reading the scene. I don't look as if I have my act together. I have last night's dress still on, and I didn't even wash the makeup off my face. I must really look a mess.

"What happened last night wasn't my fault," I say, knowing now it's time to defend my reputation. I need him to know that whatever I may look like right now, I'm no longer a screwup. "I didn't mess up. I had a party, and the wrong people showed up. That's it."

His gaze flits across my face. "I know that, Treasure Chest."

And just like that, tears burn the back of my eyes as most of the tension leaves my body.

"Thank you," I say from my heart.

The corners of Leo's mouth tease a hint of a smile. "I heard you had a great event last night. I wish your mom and I would've been invited."

My face drops as warmth flashes across my skin. I thought about inviting them. "I know. I should've."

My dad puts two fingers under my chin and gently lifts my face. "Next time?"

I nod. "Next time."

He initiates a hug, and I squeeze him tight. My dad acknowledging that last night wasn't my fault expands in my chest, filling me with contentment, making me forget how unsettled I am about Martha and Lena rummaging through my things.

"And I'm aware that moving in with Achilles isn't easy for you. But after the bad press, it has to be done."

I snort a chuckle as I decide against reciting some of the passages in *TRM*'s last post about me. In essence, my dad is right. I actually hate to admit that living with Achilles is a pretty good tactical move. Although the thought of spending time alone with Achilles Lord in the confines of his home scares the hell out of me.

"Okay," I say, acquiescing with a sigh. "I'll move in with him."

Then Leo puts his hands on my shoulders and leans back to make steady eye contact with me. "If at any second you don't feel comfortable in his home, then you call me."

I want to say that I don't feel comfortable right now, just thinking about living in the same place as Achilles. I want to complain about how mean Achilles has been to me thus far and how I can't imagine him being hospitable to me at all. But after Dad's congratulations on my adult-sized success, I don't want to whine like a little girl who wants her daddy to fix all her worries.

"Okay," I say in a voice so small that I wonder if he heard me.

"Also," he says, raising his eyebrows, "I expect you to be present at dinner tomorrow night."

Shit. How did he know I planned to skip it?

"Your grandmother's hosting it."

I gasp as my jaw drops. "Grandmother? She's in town?"

His eyebrows wrinkle in a worrisome manner. "Yes," he barely says.

I ask when she got into town and why no one told me before now, and Leo assures me that he also just learned that she's the one hosting, and whatever she wants to tell the family is supposedly very important.

Now I share my dad's worried look. "Do you think she's sick?"

Leo's expression changes from worry to something that makes him look as if he's trying to solve a complicated math equation in his head. "I don't know," he finally says. "I guess we'll learn what the hoopla is about tomorrow." He kisses me quickly on the cheek. "Just be there, Treasure Chest." He tips his head to the side as he points at me. "I mean it. Don't skip this dinner."

Moving In

TREASURE GROVE

I feel like I've been clobbered with a baseball bat, one of those plastic ones that T-ballers use, as I ride alone in the elevator up to Achilles's place. My hands fly up to the sides of my head, and my fingers massage my temples. Ooh, my headache aims to get the best of me. But I close my eyes and inhale deeply through my nostrils. I've already gotten through the process of getting checked in as a resident. They finger-printed me so that I have touch access to all the amenities, including Achilles's private gym and spa and indoor swimming pool. *How fancy.* But that's not all. I've been assigned my own parking spot in Achilles's private garage on the seventy-eighth floor.

Is Achilles home? Another wave of nausea ripples through my gut, and I inhale deeply to let the cool elevator air dissolve that sick feeling. *I hope not.*

It's Saturday. Unless he is a workaholic, which I suspect he is—all uptight people like him are—then he has to be out. Contrary to what my life has looked like since diving headfirst into renovations, I am not a workaholic. If last night's brawl hadn't happened, I would no doubt be having brunch with a few friends and then making dinner for another set of friends. I love throwing dinner parties. I fear now that I'm living with the Grinch Who Stole Happiness, I won't be able to host as much.

I hug myself tightly as chills climb up and down my arms. After my dad left, I accepted the fact that I'm not feeling so well. It's common for me to become stress sick, and after the month I've had, I think that is what's happening to me. If I'm going to be bright-eyed and bushy-tailed for tomorrow night's dinner, then I'll need to go to bed early tonight. But that's going to be impossible. I'm too nervous. I am not ready to see Achilles.

Maybe he's out to brunch with his girlfriend,

or boyfriend. People are really puzzled about which sex he prefers. His sexuality has been in question for many years. I never paid attention to the rumors because I never felt the need to. Not until Paisley started up with Hercules did I have to think about another Lord brother. But Achilles has never been seen in public with a woman who isn't his mother or with a man unless it's one of his brothers. Personally, I think he's been subject to unfair scrutiny. When a man who looks like him isn't womanizing or spruced up with the love of his life, then people go looking for a reason why he's not shoving himself into a box. His looks are top shelf—chiseled jawline, sensual mouth, and bedroom eyes that can peer into your soul. But by the way he's treated me thus far, I can seriously understand why he's single. He's a storm cloud, and nobody wants to be rained on every day of their lives.

The groan that gets trapped in my throat has almost become a sob when the elevator comes to a stop. *I'm not ready yet*, I think as I stare at my reflection in the gold-paneled walls as they slide open. Dark semicircles invade the skin under my red eyes. I have that walking-dead-like appearance, not vivacious at all.

"Please don't be home," I say with a heartfelt whisper. Admittedly, I don't want him to see me this way.

The doors finish opening, but my feet stay glued to the elevator's floor. I'm waiting to be closed inside again. Maybe I can go home and sleep in my bed for the night. I could use the familiarity. Especially since I don't feel so well. I cough into my balled fist, and the sound carries through what appears to be a foyer.

My burning eyes blink at the golden-yellow and white chevron travertine marble floors. They're quite stunning, and expensive. I know this because I considered using them in the restaurant. Although the stone is very pretty, it's not reasonable for high foot traffic. But still, it's so peaceful beyond the elevator car. It's as if time has been frozen stiff. Without giving it another thought, I step out onto the marble floor and look up. *Wow, the ceiling is so high and domed*, reminding me of a glass birdcage.

"Hello," I call, and my voice echoes back to me.

Journeying farther out, I take note that to my right lingers a spiraling staircase that leads to a second level. I turn left, and the view makes me wince as I grow tense. A tall wall made of glass gives me the willies. I gape at the hazy sky layered with warm, humid clouds. They seem to be watching, as if they know they're making me uncomfortable. I never liked being this far off the ground. When we were kids, my dad took Lynx and me to the Eiffel Tower, and the whole time, I clung to Leo's long leg like a cat avoiding water. That fear is the reason my parents never bought an apartment similar to this one. I would've never felt a moment of peace.

Unfortunately, that queasy sensation is back in my stomach. The only thing that stops me from throwing up all over Achilles's expensive marble floor is the fact that I haven't eaten since yesterday. Also, my attention has been newly stolen by a spotless glass case that resembles a fish tank. Inside, there's a strange object which looks to be glowing while suspended in thin air.

I move closer to the case as if it's a hypnotist's charm drawing me to itself. My head snaps to a tilt when I figure out what it is. The light emerging from a silver pen forces me to squint.

"What in the world…," I mutter.

"Welcome, Miss Grove," a woman says.

I jump and spin on my heels to look into the

eyes of a slender woman who's wearing an off-white button-front shirt with a green khaki skirt and black orthopedic shoes. Her expression lacks even a hint of a smile. She would be creepy if her features weren't so soft and beautiful.

"Hi," I say in a choked whisper, and I close the distance between us with an outstretched hand.

Without hesitation, the woman shakes my hand. "Hello, I'm Caroline. I'm here to get you settled."

"Is Mr. Lord home?" I realize I'm not only still holding her hand, but I'm squeezing it in anticipation of her answer, so I quickly let go.

"No, Miss Grove."

I sigh with relief. "I'm Treasure. Please, call me Treasure."

"Yes, Treasure," Caroline says, and I think I see a faint smile building at the corners of her mouth.

It's a relief to see a change in her dutiful expression. Her tiny smile sort of makes me feel as if my feet are back on the ground—so much so that I'm suddenly aware that I'm wearing a party dress with a pair of closed-toe sandals. After my dad informed me that I would be moving in with

Achilles, I felt so anxious that I couldn't do anything but pack up and get it over with already. So I didn't shower, change my clothes, or wash off my smudged makeup.

"Where is he?" I ask, hoping she'll say something like "the Bermuda Triangle."

"He's working today."

Ha! It's just as I thought. He's a workaholic. I'm itching to ask Caroline if she knows why there's a pen floating in a glass box, but my cell phone rings, so instead, I ask her to excuse me as I take my device out of my purse.

Viewing the name on the screen, my grin stretches from ear to ear. "Brooklyn!" I say into the device.

"What time is dinner?"

I quirk an eyebrow. "Dinner?"

"The old gang. Dinner. You don't remember?"

My eyes grow wide. "What? One sec." I shuffle through my phone apps and select my calendar. Dang it. It's written in black and white with a pink tag to remind me. Dinner with my old reality show cast members at my apartment tonight. I had forgotten all about it.

I turn to Caroline. There's a hint of curiosity

in her eyes, and it seems she's on standby, prepared to do whatever I ask of her. I'm certain that Achilles wants me to make myself at home in his penthouse. Well, if I were at home, feeling achy and all, I would pull it together and have dinner with my friends.

But for some reason, something deep inside shoots my focus over to Achilles's glass-encased pen. A man who keeps something like that in the foyer is sending a certain message.

"Treasure?" Brooklyn asks.

"Yeah, I'm still here." I should tell her we have to postpone.

"Oh, and we heard about your engagement to Achilles Lord."

I stifle a gasp as my eyes grow wide, and a lump the size of a bowling ball expands in my stomach. "Oh," I say, pretending to be cheery.

"You're living with him, right?"

"Huh?"

"Why all the secrecy, girlfriend? Are we having dinner at his house?"

Say no, say no, say no...

"Because we also heard what happened last night at the restaurant. It's sort of a surprise, because didn't you have this big blowout with the brother, Orion…"

"Okay, dinner here tonight at my new place. I mean, Achilles's penthouse," I say to keep her from inquiring about Orion. I don't want to talk about him ever again.

"Oh, so then, you do live with him?"

I paste a faker-than-fake smile on while looking at Caroline and say, "I'm engaged to him, aren't I?"

The Perfect Ex

ACHILLES LORD

"Why do you keep checking your watch?" Nero, my cousin, asks.

The hairs on my arms stand at attention. Treasure Grove should be at my apartment by now. Caroline will get her situated. I've asked Barbara Townsend, the private chef that my brothers and I share, to make lunch at three and then dinner at seven. I've been toying with the decision to stay in a hotel tonight. I need more time to prepare to have her in my personal space.

Shit, I've already forgotten what he asked.

"What did you say?"

Nero's eyebrows ruffle with concern. "What's wrong with you, Achilles?"

I sit up straight, forcing my head back into our conversation. "Nothing. What were you saying about Xander and Leo?"

He doesn't drop his look of curiosity about my state of mind, but I give him an answering grimace that says *Mind your own business*. Taking the hint, Nero raises his glass of whiskey to his lips. "I was saying that if Yash can't locate what we're looking for, then there's a reason it's hidden." He takes swig of whiskey and screws his face as he feels the burn. "I don't even like this shit."

"Then why are you drinking it?"

Nero flashes a dismissive frown. "I need it to get through this conversation," he mumbles then readjusts in his seat. "I was saying that if we hedge our bets in trusting the Grove brothers, then we might as well just pull our pants down and bend over."

I grunt at the unsightly visual. "Of course I don't trust them. But what about her?"

His head seems to float as he leans back and says, "Treasure?"

I shrug as I take a quick swig of my own whiskey, wincing from the burn.

"Funny thing about her. It seems your future wife was broker than a joke before agreeing to the deal." He snorts facetiously while smirking. "I'm not surprised Leo would strip his daughter of cash and then pimp her out to the highest bidder."

"I haven't bid on her," I spit, the words leaving my mouth just as bitter as they taste.

"I know that. I'm just saying."

"I know what you were saying, but the fact that she was broke is news to me. Tell me more about that."

His eyebrows quirk up as he takes a moment to assess my mood. My expression stays steady, urging him to get on with it. My cousin has ways which can be annoying to most but not to me—he is who is, and that's it.

Nero stretches his neck from side to side as he wraps his fingers around his glass of whiskey and looks at the dingy brown liquid as if he's thinking twice about drinking more. "We tracked her financials back ten years. She hadn't received any trust payments since then. Treasure Grove has been doing it all by herself. That restaurant almost sunk her battleship. She was in debt up to here before she agreed to marry you for the money." He shakes a finger as though he's amused by whatever he's going to say next. "She's gotten paid recently, and not from the family chest. Tuff Studios paid her a few million."

"For the TV show," I say, recalling the gossip about her filming with Simon Linney on location. That's where he cheated on her with that actress whose name escapes me. I hate that I know that, but a woman who's an object of celebrity gossip is going to be my wife, so I have to know it.

Nero's eyes are shining as if what he has to say next only gets better. "Yeah, but she's been using the money from Tuff to live on. After renovating her restaurant, she hadn't touched the trust money."

I throw my hands up, not getting the punchline.

Nero leans toward me as if he's letting me in on a secret. "You do know that she has an out, don't you?"

I didn't know that, and that's exactly what my scowl conveys.

"If she's able to pay back what she spent from the trust, she can say *sayonara* to the marriage contract she signed."

My trachea feels like it's squeezing my breaths.

I'm slightly relieved her father and uncle wrote in an out for her, but then I'm not. "How did that get past you?"

He sighs. "It didn't. Herc agreed to it last minute. It was the only way that deal would get done. Treasure's mother insisted on the clause last minute."

"Her mother?" I spit. "What the hell does her mother have to do with it?"

Nero laughs with an edge. "Has it been so long, Cousin?"

Ignoring Nero's comment about how long it's been—we both know it hasn't been that long—I narrow an eye at him as I stroke my chin, trying to figure out if Treasure's the kind of person who would take what she needs and say "fuck you" to the rest of us, including her family. They cut her off. She may have no real loyalty to them. "Shit," I mutter and then gulp another swallow of liquor. The burn numbs my anger and keeps me from exploding at Nero about adding that clause without my permission. "What's our plan B?" I ask, still wincing from the sting in my throat.

"Achilles, is that you?" a feminine and highly curious voice asks.

My muscles lock as I snap my attention

toward whoever said that. *Damn it.* It's too late to stop myself from gaping at my ex, Penelope Garner. I haven't seen her in so long. But she's still beautiful. Her dark hair, flawless skin, and large, seductive eyes still threaten to slay me.

"What are you doing here?" The words leave my mouth unfiltered. If I were thinking, I would've chosen a different tone, one that didn't make me seem unready to see her. But she's wearing a skirt suit, the kind that reminds me of a pillbox for some reason. Penelope is an interior designer, and she works a lot of weekends since her high-end clientele are at the office during the week.

Her thumb trembles as she points it over her shoulder. "I was in the neighborhood."

The neighborhood? Nero and I pass each other a look. We chose this dive because it's downtown, far away from Penelope's Upper East Side scene. I would ask her what's she doing in this area, but it's not my place. We're not together anymore because she couldn't—no, wouldn't—wait for me to sort out getting Hercules married so that my family could earn a financial benefit from the Lord family trust. Of course, Herc didn't end up marrying our cousin. I was working up the nerve to contact Penelope as soon as Orion was securely contracted to marry Treasure. But then Treasure refused to marry him, and I was the last Lord standing.

But I always figured that as far as my future wife goes, Penelope was the right choice. She has an old-money pedigree and wears the outfits to match. Her roots can be traced all the way back to the Carnegies. Not only that, but she has grace. Sure, she can be stuck-up at times, but that's because she's a serious person, just as I am.

But then there's Treasure Grove...

I snap myself out of a daze. One of Nero's eyes is slitted. He's sending me a message, telling me that being seen with Penelope is a problem and I should resolve it, fast. Only a few people know that she and I were involved, Nero being one of them and Orion the other. She closes the distance between us to stand close to my right shoulder. I gently inhale the familiar scent of her floral perfume. I used to love this woman, once upon a time. She's the only woman I've ever loved.

"How have you been?" I find enough breath to say.

"Fine, and you?" Her tone is vulnerable, hopeful.

I nod swiftly.

"Oh, I heard about your good news. Congratulations." Her solemn expression holds hope that I'll denounce the press release that went out at ten this morning.

I clear my throat and look away from her glossy eyes as I say, "Thank you."

"And Treasure Grove, no less." She sounds impressed, and I would believe her act if her voice hadn't cracked just a little.

"What about you?" I have to change the subject. "How's life been treating you?"

She blinks at me for a few beats and then whispers, "Fine." Her voice is shaky, so I know she is not fine.

The news of my engagement to Treasure has hurt her. The truth would make her feel better, but unfortunately, I can't tell her the truth.

Nero clears his throat, and we both glance at him until our magnetic energy forces our eyes back on each other. Do I still love her? I'm not certain. I feel something for her, though, but whatever that is doesn't spoil how I feel about Treasure Grove moving into my penthouse.

I shift my finger, pointing between me and Nero. "I apologize," I say. "We're in a—"

"No, it's fine. I'm fine. I'm mean, it's fine," she says, cutting me off. Penelope takes two steps back. "Good seeing you, Achilles." Her voice cracks again.

She quickly turns her back on me and hurries out of the bar. I know Penelope well, and she wants me to follow her. But I can't. Not this time.

Nero and I gape at each other. I think we're both asking ourselves the same question.

"What's she doing south of Fourteenth Street?" Nero asks in a lawyer-like tone that's teeming with suspicion.

"I don't know. Do you think she came looking for me?"

He regards me shrewdly. "And how would she know you'd be here? This isn't your kind of place either."

I take note of the muddy-brown shiplap walls, the dull-green carpet, and the red cracked fake leather chairs. The only reason we're in this place is because it's Saturday and we wanted to meet somewhere not so crowded where two men can have a drink and a greasy steak. And furthermore, I hadn't known this bar existed. Nero suggested it.

We ate first, and the steak was terrible, and so is the whiskey.

"You think she has you on GPS?" Nero asks with a cynical laugh.

"Nah." In my denial, I sound sure of myself, but I do have my suspicions. Orion knew I'd be out with Nero. Nah, he couldn't have told her where to find us. I think it's a coincidence. She could have a client who bought a fixer-upper in the neighborhood. Before Penelope and I parted ways, I made her a promise. Even though we had broken up because she couldn't be certain that I, rather than Hercules, wouldn't end up marrying a distant cousin, I promised her that she was the only woman I'd ever love. I'm marrying Treasure Grove, but that doesn't mean my promise has been broken. I run through memories of Treasure Grove—how it felt being alone in the elevator with her, and the thrill that shot up my arm when my hand grazed hers while signing the contract.

I flinch when Nero smacks the bar twice and then waves a hand at the bartender. "Just give me a goddamn Coke."

Readjusting on my bar stool, I'm forced to refocus on what's important at the moment, and that's Penelope surprisingly showing up to our meeting.

Did Orion…

Nah…

Did he?

New Digs

TREASURE GROVE

I've just been asked to take off my shoes and put them on a contraption that's part coat-tree and part shoe rack. I've never been in such a sanitized environment in my life. There's not a lick of dust anywhere. Every room that Caroline shows me looks as if no one has ever lived in it. And Achilles has more artifacts on display than the MoMA which is just down the street and around the corner. In the room he uses as a den, he has gorgeous sculptures made from twisted metal placed decoratively around the expensive white furniture. In another sitting room, I count four unfinished limestone sculptures of the human anatomy—like a torso, a leg and hip, a man's back, and two feet, each attached to a calf.

These sculptures are encased in glass just like the pen is. And each attempt at completion is signed by a different artist. The pieces are so odd that it makes me wonder if I should worry about living with a man who seems to have an infatuation with imprisoning limestone body parts and a writing pen in glass.

When I ask Caroline if she knows why he has all of those undone sculptures, she says she doesn't know, and I actually believe her. Achilles is certainly a mystery. He could actually be the true-life depiction of that guy in *American Psycho*. I should watch my back, lock my bedroom door, and steer clear of him.

She shows me more rooms, like a library, Achilles's office, my office, a bar, and several other rooms that are too immaculate to ever use. And then, finally, Caroline takes me to the kitchen, which is the only space I care about other than the one I'll sleep in. One look, and all of my worries about the weird guy I'm now living with fade into the background like white noise. As a restauranteur, my eyes gravitate first to the built-in Viking wall ovens and then to the double cooktops in the middle of a massive white stone-topped island. I admire one of two Bertazzoni double refrigerators—there's one on each end of this true chef's kitchen.

"This is very nice," I say, running my hand against the flush gray cabinets. The wood is as soft as butter. "Does he have a private chef?" I ask, knowing that a man like him would.

I turn to look at Caroline. Her fingers are clasped dutifully and pressed against her abdomen. She almost looks unreal, reminding me of one of those servants to rich men I've seen portrayed in movies. That's it… she seems two-dimensional. I wonder if there's more to her.

"Today, yes," she says. "But usually, Achilles makes his own meals, or he'll order from twenty-four-hour room service. You have access to that service as well." She bends her arm to scowl at her wristwatch and then tells me that Barbara Townsend, the family's chef, will be in by three o'clock to cook lunch and then dinner later.

Oddly, disappointment snakes around my heart, feeling like a chilly breeze in my chest. "Only for me?" I ask as I finally admit to myself that deep down inside, I would actually like to see Achilles's face. I want to verify that stab of attraction I felt for him the last time we saw each other.

"Yes, Treasure," Caroline says.

I smile because even though my first name sounds odd leaving her lips, but still, I'm happy she used it instead of Miss Grove. Not even my employees call me Miss Grove. Then suddenly, what she said a few seconds ago finally absorbs in my brain. "Wait, do you mean *the* Barbara Townsend?"

The smooth skin of Caroline's forehead wrinkles and then evens out again, as if she was unsure how to answer my question. Talking fast, I give her a history lesson on Townsend's career as a head chef in some of the world's most famous restaurants, brought to an end by a car accident in Miami that nearly killed her. When I mention she walks with a slight limp, Caroline confirms that we are talking about the same person.

"Wow, the Lords nabbed her. Good for them," I say, nodding, impressed.

Caroline's expression remains inscrutable. No wonder she has no lines on her face and a full head of gray hair. Her face rarely makes lines of expression. *How old is she anyway?*

"Well," I say, running the tips of my fingers across a cabinet again. I catch Caroline staring at my hand with concern. I bet Achilles can't tolerate finger smudges. It's also hard to imagine him cooking his own meals. I call bullshit on that. Of course, Caroline has no reason to lie to me, but I still call bullshit.

However, since Caroline looks so disturbed by my flagrant touching, I drop my hand and tell her that there's no need for Barbara to cook for me today or tonight.

Caroline draws back as though I just unleashed a string of profanity on her. "Excuse me?"

I'm a little reluctant to tell her my plans for the night, but I have to tell her because I'll be cooking dinner in her boss's precious kitchen. "I'm having friends over, and although Barbara is a very talented chef, I alone do the cooking when I host friends for dinner."

Caroline gapes at me as if she's pondering all the reasons why I should rethink my plan.

"Is Achilles joining us?" I ask. "Because I can cook for him too." I figure that's the reason for her hesitation.

She shakes her head stiffly. "No, I don't believe he'll be home for dinner."

My eyebrows shoot up. So he is smartly keeping his distance, delaying the inevitable. I lower my eyebrows with a sigh of relief. "Okay, then, I'll make dinner tonight, and please, would you join us?"

"Umm…"

I think she's about to decline my invitation until I say, "I sure would like to get to know you better."

First, she's silent, and then with a tiny shrug of her shoulders, as if she's weighed the pros and cons and arrived at a definite answer, she says, "Yes, I'll join you, Treasure."

She sounds so awkward referring to me as Treasure that I almost let her off the hook and say that she's free to go back to calling me Miss Grove if she's more comfortable with it. But I don't.

Next, Caroline guides me to our final destination—my "sleeping quarters" is what she calls it.

"So how long have you worked for Mr. Lord?" I ask as we finish climbing a spiral staircase, shamelessly prying.

"Twenty-seven years," she replies proudly.

My mouth falls open. I did not expect her to

say that. "Twenty-seven years? You're under no obligation to answer, but how old are you?"

"Fifty-seven," she says rather confidently and without pause.

I gasp. Fifty-seven is twenty-six years older than I am. Achilles isn't that much older than I am. He must've been five or six when she first started working for the Lords.

"Wow, beauty gods, how many goats do I have to sacrifice to look like her at fifty-seven?"

Caroline's mild chuckle resonates from deep in her throat. Even her laugh is uptight, but I think she's flattered.

Admiring her flawless profile, I say, "Well, you are very beautiful, Caroline."

Looking down, she blushes a gorgeous shade of dusty rose. "Thank you, and so are you."

I thank her as we venture down another wide hallway with ivory travertine marble floors. A glass wall is to our right, and a breathtaking horseshoe view of the park outlined by the sort of buildings that make this city one of a kind is plastered down below for my viewing enjoyment. Even still, my head battles a severe case of vertigo that wants to overcome me. I simply don't know how long I can live this high off the ground and maintain my sanity. I mean, really, is it truly healthy for a human being to live this far away from God's green earth? I think not.

We stop in front of two massive white wooden doors, which have the most gorgeous rippled casing outlining them. They look more like the entrance to a palace than to a bedroom.

Caroline turns the golden knobs and pushes. Now that I see the interior, I'm unable to mask my gasp. Crossing the threshold, I let my gaze roam the room. The king-sized bed is made up with a spotless white duvet and large fluffy matching pillows. A crystal-encrusted spherical pendant light spills a soft, inviting orange glow across the bed. The relaxing atmosphere makes me yawn. If I wasn't so excited to cook dinner for my friends, I would do what I probably should anyway and strip out of all my clothes and climb into bed. My body is past empty, and I'm seriously running on fumes. But still, as long as I can keep driving the car, I will.

"And this is your parlor," Caroline says, elegantly pointing a hand to the step-down seating area.

My eyes take in an L-shaped blue velvet sofa facing an extremely large flat-screen television.

There's also a white marble round table with four high-backed leather chairs on one side of the room along with my own little stocked wet bar and glass refrigerator full of all sorts of snacks. Caroline shows me how the TV folds in and out of a pocket in the ceiling.

"It feels like he intends to trap me in my room," I say with a nervous laugh. I'm only half joking.

"No," Caroline says, shaking her head adamantly. "You are free to use any part of the house you like."

I search her face for signs that she has no idea what she's talking about and is merely speculating. After all, she hasn't seen the way he treated me when he and I last saw each other. Regardless, I smile tightly and nod, my way of letting her know that I'll try to believe her.

I walk back up the steps to the main sleeping area and finish looking around. There's still a lot to take in. I like the wall featured behind the headboard. It's made of some sort of smooth gray stone. Then there are the floating end tables on each side of the bed, both with chrome tops and trimmed with white wood. Two standing floor lamps match the pendant light to help create the cozy ambiance that wants to lure me to sleep.

"So, does he have his own interior designer?" I ask Caroline, sliding my fingers down the stone wall feature.

"No," she says, sounding slightly surprised by my question.

Nodding, impressed, I give my room another once-over. "Then he put all of this together himself?"

"Yes, he did."

A question locked in my head wants out as my lips quirk up into an impish smile.

Surprisingly, Caroline regards me with a smile so faint it could be missed. I think she's intrigued by the look on my face.

I should ask…

I'll ask.

"Is he gay?" falls out of my mouth like an apple dropping from a tree to the ground—*plop*.

"Oh!" Caroline gasps, leaning away from me. It's clear she's shocked by my question. Or maybe she's shocked that I asked it. That's right—she thinks we're a couple. Everybody does thanks to *TRM*.

I wave my blunder away with my hands.

"Sorry, forget I asked that." I fake smile. "He's my fiancé. Of course he's not gay." My chuckle is awkward, forced, and I'm sure it matches my flushed face.

"No, he is not," Caroline answers in a voice void of judgment.

My nod is so stiff as my eyes dart around the room, reaching for anything and everything but her face. *Gosh, why did I ask that question?*

Enough seconds of silence go by to place our interaction in the past. Time bears down on me. I'll have to go to the kitchen soon, get a feel for where things are, see what's already in the refrigerator, and then come up with a plan for dinner.

Smiling cordially, I set my focus back on Caroline. "And my clothes and things are already here?"

"Yes," she says, her dutiful tone not missing a beat and eyes locked on me.

Then I follow her to my closet, which is vast and elegant. People spend a lot of money to get these sorts of closets built. Every single article of clothing I own hangs neatly on one of several bars. Furthermore, shirts are with shirts, pants with pants, and so forth, and each garment is color coordinated. She shows me how my underwear and other garments are folded neatly in dresser drawers by kind and arranged by color. My shoes, hats, purses and scarves, and jewelry have also been displayed with care.

I stay silent while Caroline reveals my closet to me like a museum tour guide. This is all too much. If it were up to me, I would've packed one suitcase. That way, if I wanted, I could easily go wee-wee-wee all the way home. But look at this closet. I can't go anywhere. I'm too dug in.

The Lady of My House

ACHILLES LORD

ELEVEN HOURS LATER

"What the…"

I step out of the elevator and into my penthouse. The lighting in the foyer is brighter than usual. Seeing the change, a bitter taste rushes into my mouth. I bend my stiff neck from one side to the other and then grunt painfully. *How could Caroline let this happen?* I clap twice, pause, then clap two more times to make the ambiance more to my liking, which is dim and relaxed, the way I like to feel when I come home from a long day of work.

Treasure Grove must've browbeat Caroline

into getting her way. I instructed Caroline to make sure she's comfortable but not at the expense of how things around here should be.

I clench my jaw tightly and tug down on my tie, loosening it. That's better, even though I'm still tense through my shoulders. I probably should've gone to the Four Seasons as planned. After Nero and I left Niles Bar, we went back to my office and held a conference call with James, our finance guy, and Hercules. Everybody had a job to do: find our side's advantage in that damn contract I signed, any advantage beyond the obvious, the big payoff of seeing through this sham of a union long enough to have the original trust legally and permanently transferred into my name, since I'm the eldest son. It's a large-scale power play. If all goes well, it'll set my family up securely and comfortably for the rest of our lives. As for the rest of the Lord descendants, none of them will have to jump through our great-great-grandfather's puritanical hoops again. I will abolish all the rules and regulations that each descendent has to satisfy to even receive minimum payments. No more marrying cousins either. That shit will be over with.

Night fell, and we still couldn't find anything

that could help us stop Treasure from paying her family back and nullifying the contract. At least as of now, Treasure is the only person who can blow up our deal. She'll have to be managed. And as far as looking like we're in love, she and I will have to put on the show of shows, at least in public. Nero suggested we get help and gave me the name of a top relationship expert who works with entertainment agents and publicists. She helps Hollywood couples put together for the sake of publicity stunts to appear as if they're in love in real life.

I jump when I hear an eruption of voices that sound like women laughing. I stand still and incline an ear in their direction. In my vanity dining room, I hear a high-pitched rumble of chattering and chuckling. No one's supposed to be sitting in that area.

What the hell—is she having a party?

I smell food. Barbara must have made dinner already, but dinner was supposed to be served at seven. It's now—I check the time on my Swiss watch—almost eleven. Dinner should be over, the kitchen clean, and my...

One of the women is singing. *What the hell.* Treasure is having a party.

I take off my suit jacket and hang it on the coat-tree evenly positioned between the two chrome-plated elevator doors. Then I see the women's shoes. There are five pairs, all but one are high heels. The sandals with the silver studs— I bet those are hers. They look like something she'd wear, edgy and unserious.

Where's Caroline, anyway?

The singing ends with a dramatic note and is followed by clapping. Annoyance makes me hurry up and take off my shoes. Somebody's high heels are in my spot. That puts a sour taste in my mouth too.

I head toward the noise they're keeping up. But I stop in my tracks when I'm halfway down the corridor and tip my head back to look up. The beams emanating from the chrome pendant lights are too bright. *Did she mess with those lights too?* Is this what I have to look forward to? I clap twice, pause, then clap again. The lighting dims, just the way I like it.

After I take a few more steps, one of the women's voices comes in clearly when she says, "But Cherry Attwell, she's not a girl's girl, even though she plays one on TV."

"Although she may have just done you a

favor," another woman says. "Simon Linney, Achilles Lord? Umm… I'm sorry, but excellent snag, Treasure."

My arm flies up to rub my chest but stops halfway as the conversation continues.

"Yeah, he's hot as hell but very strange." That's a third voice.

"I heard he may not be into women."

"That's just a rumor, right, Caroline?" *That's Treasure.*

My hand completes the journey to rub my tight chest. *Caroline? She's with them?*

Caroline doesn't say anything, but why would Treasure confirm my sexuality with her? Have they discussed my sexuality in the past? My eyebrows raise and stay high. For a moment, my anger subsides, and I want to hear more.

"Shanique, thank you for freestyling my own personal breakup song. I'll take it to the grave with me. You still got it, gorgeous. And to the rest of you, chill out already. I haven't seen him in over a month."

I wait to hear a reply to the last part of what Treasure has said, but it's deathly silent, and the quietness feels like the wrong brand of silence. And then someone says, "You haven't seen your *fiancé* in over a month?" She put emphasis on the word "fiancé."

This time, the awkward silence belongs to Treasure, which is my cue to bring an end to their conversation.

Hairs stand up on the back of my neck as I stride into their gathering. I stop when, like a gust of wind, all eyes land on me. There are six women at my table. The count includes Treasure and Caroline, who quickly stands as if she's been caught doing something wrong. Of course, Caroline could never do anything wrong in my eyes. She practically raised me.

"Achilles," Caroline says as her gaze dart around my face. "Your coat."

I raise a hand to settle her nerves. "It's no problem. I hung it up."

I take a sweeping glance at all the amused expressions that are locked on me. They've made themselves comfortable at my Anthony Lithgow custom-made table and Bulan Minx leatherback chairs. Where's the bowl of solid silver fruit that has been mindfully placed in the middle of the table beneath a pendant light that has layers of rose petals made of silver? Every day, the table has sat perfectly clean and undisturbed, with the fruit glowing pristinely, until now.

"Look who's late for dinner," one of the ladies, who's made herself overly comfortable in my chair, says. There are four unfamiliar faces watching me, each wearing a gratified grin. All of a sudden, I'm hot under the collar and undo another button of my shirt. That doesn't quell the heat or make me look away from the guarded and very sexy, and piercing eyes that belong to Treasure Grove.

"Caroline, please, sit back down and take a load off," she says, not taking her eyes off me. "If there's anything Mr. Lord needs, then I'll be happy to fetch it for him."

My eyes narrow some more. She's beautiful tonight, although a little dark under the eyes. Has she been sleeping? I bet she doesn't take care of herself very well. I wonder if she's well, but I'm also bothered by the hostile way she said "fetch it." I find her tone unnerving but a bit of a turn-on too. Nobody talks to me that way, nobody. And for a fragment of a second, I visualize her bent over the edge of my custom-made table, my hands squeezing her hips as I get an eyeful of her flawless ass while slamming my cock inside of her, then I'd back out of her, bit by bit, feeling every sensation of the ride, before slamming inside her again, hard and punishing.

Shit.

"That's a good idea, Treasure. Fetch whatever he wants. Like, fetch it," says one of her friends. I force my eyes off the woman I really want to fuck right now to glare at the woman with the long blond braids. She's brazenly flirting with her eyes in a way that's too excessive to take seriously.

The other ladies, blowing out their cheeks, restrain giggles. This is odd. It's all too damn odd.

Treasure shakes her head as a beautiful rose color burns into her cheeks.

"I don't need anything," I bark, mostly embarrassed but angry too. She should've asked before inviting guests though. "Enjoy your dinner, Caroline." Well, the end of dinner. Their plates are empty and wineglasses half full. Did they disturb my *Mes Fleur Collection?*

"Treasure, aren't you going to introduce your old friends to your new squeeze?" the woman with the blond braids asks.

"Why don't you join us for a drink, Achilles Lord?" says another blonde with a short haircut. The woman leering at me looks familiar.

"I think they should kiss, at least. Show us they're *really* in love," the beautiful one with billows of curly brown hair says. But there's a hint of cynicism in her voice.

"Okay," Treasure says glibly as she bounds to her feet.

I'm unable to move as she makes her approach. Her tight jeans make her long, shapely legs sexy. She's wearing an oversized white T-shirt with the words *Mind Me* across the front. The hem of her shirt doesn't extend past the waistband of her jeans. The subtle swinging of her hips is sexy. I swallow, unable to rip my eyes off of her.

She's in front of me. Her gorgeous eyes widen in a sexually alluring manner, fastening on mine. I'm too overwhelmed by the rich vanilla scent and the energetic heat that's coming off her body. I'm hard. I grow harder when she presses her hands on my torso and rises a few inches higher. I suspect she's standing on her tiptoes.

My mouth falls open as her breaths press against my lips. She wants in. I quirk an eyebrow, knowing I want to but wondering if I should. Then her friends' amused murmurs slip through the air around us. And now we have to do it. Her lips are on mine, and I let my mouth join the kiss.

The red wine that she tastes like might explain why she's chosen to prove our relationship with this kiss. Things are happening in my chest that have never happened to me. Her tongue is addictive and incredibly soft. It takes everything in me to keep my cool. I fight the urge to weave my fingers through her belt loops and bring her against my cock. Our tongues stroke and rub. Our lips weave and press. I want to cup one of her cone-shaped tits. She's not wearing a bra. The fucking longing makes me moan, and then she moans into my mouth too. Her fingers are in my hair, touching my scalp. Shit, that's my hot spot.

I step back and away from her.

A Kiss Isn't Just a Kiss

TREASURE GROVE

I can't believe I did that. In a daze, I stare into his eyes as my friends clap and hoot. I cannot tear my eyes away from the look on his face. His frown can't become more intense than it is now. I think I've thoroughly shocked him. But he kissed back like he enjoyed it. I enjoyed it. I'm still enjoying it. The floating feeling in my head is subsiding, but still... wow. I am on cloud nine.

But now he looks as if he's ready to clobber me. His narrowed eyes and pressed lips make my insides recoil, which reminds me that before I kissed him, I felt like crap.

I'm seriously on my last leg. My energy has

been up and down. For instance, after Caroline left me alone to make myself comfortable, I showered in the spa-sized shower, and the steam had relieved some of my stress-cold symptoms, only to make me want to crawl into bed afterward. But no, I couldn't. I had dinner to make.

While cooking, a serious jolt of adrenaline caused me to feel a lot better. At first, I didn't believe Achilles actually cooked for himself, until I searched through his stocked refrigerators and found every single item I needed to make a mad *bistec encebollado*—steak and onions, a Puerto Rican dish that my head chef, Nya, taught me. Before I dashed off to Iceland to make enough money to save my restaurant, Nya used to teach me how to cook a new dish every Wednesday night. Her bistec encebollado blew me away.

The scent that wafted from Achilles's kitchen even lured Caroline out from wherever she was hiding in the house. Her grandmother was Puerto Rican and used to make the dish for their family on the third Sunday of every month. I gave her a taste of my version. Remaining loyal to her grandmother, Caroline wouldn't confirm or deny that my bistec encebollado was better. We had a good laugh about it. Her continuing to open up to me, to show me her human side, makes living here easier. However, she was impressed by how I could cook a full meal while keeping the kitchen clean. I confessed that my grandmother, who refused to allow servants cook her meals or clean her house as long as she was capable of doing both, taught me to clean as I go.

Luckily, my friends arrived while I was setting the table. My body didn't have enough downtime to remind me that I'm not feeling so hot. Then we sat down to eat. Of course, Caroline joined us.

Questions about Achilles and my relationship started coming at me like baseballs from a pitching machine. The first was, how did Achilles and I meet? I bullshitted my way through that one with an answer that was essentially a nonanswer. I can't even remember what I said, something about Achilles dining at my restaurant. Thankfully we started drinking wine early because I'm pretty sure a lot of my answers were suspect. But the more questions I had to dodge, the more off-color I felt. But I also loved having my girlfriends over as we caught up on each other's recent endeavors. Although they wouldn't abandon the subject of my love life.

When we landed on the subject of Achilles

and my nonexistent sex life, I was able to at least keep the topic PG-13 by remarking that Caroline practically raised Achilles. It was also a great topic of diversion because like myself, my friends couldn't believe Caroline was old enough to be a mother figure to Achilles. Questions about him as a child flew at her. But not even a couple of sips of wine could make Caroline reveal too much. She never lost any of her professionalism. Her answers remained short and not fleshed out.

I, however, at one point, told a whopper of a lie that was too much for even me. I said that Achilles spread rose petals on the bed the first time we made love. Caroline looked at me with a peculiar frown. It was as if she knew I was lying because what I explained was nowhere in his wheelhouse.

Knowing that she knew I was lying through my teeth brought back that sinking feeling in my body. I was mentally drained and tired of making shit up, and then Achilles showed up. Then, Shanique made a comment about how I should kiss my fiancé. All dinner long, she was eyeing me askew, as if she barely believed my lies. She wanted to test me, and so I did it.

And now here we are, Achilles and I, still trapped in each other's eyes. Every part of my body feels deprived of him. Our kiss was more than a simple joke. It was real. It was the sort of making out people do while on their way to second base. However, I wish I could've explained to him why I had to do it before I followed through with it.

I drop my face to end this staring thing that Achilles and I have going. My eyes skim over his crotch, and I swear he's got a bulge as big as the Rock of Gibraltar. Or maybe I'm seeing things simply because my focus is off.

"Good night, ladies," Achilles says as I try to find the right expression before facing my friends again. When I bring my eyes back up to his face, I'm relieved that he's no longer scowling. "Good night, Treasure."

The word "good night" escapes me without my actually sensing that I've said it.

It's odd how buoyant my head feels and how light I am on my feet as I float back to my chair. *Get it together, Treasure.* It was just a stupid kiss, one that was as fake as the reason why I'm living here in the first place. Forcing the corners of my mouth up, but not too high, I settle on a self-assured grin. My former castmates watch me, each with her own version of a giddy expression.

"What?" I say, feeling as though I want to melt into the comfortable chair. I think that kiss zapped all the strength I had left.

"That was hot," Claire says and then balls her fist over her mouth to yawn.

"Now I'm all hot and bothered," Summer remarks as she excessively fans herself with her fingers. She scoots her chair back. "Ben's going to get lucky tonight."

Chuckles mingle with the sound of wood sliding against marble as my guests progress through the stages of rising from their seats. Usually, we would keep company until the wee hours of the morning. But nobody expected Achilles to show up, not even Caroline. His appearance took all of us so high that now we're all crashing. Also, that red wine was not only delicious but quick.

Caroline is the first to excuse herself from the table. I think she's on her way to find Achilles and explain why I have four friends in his penthouse. I walk the others to the elevator, smiling sheepishly as they share their plans for the upcoming week, desperately trying to forget the feel and taste of my tongue entangling with Achilles's and his lips on my lips. Bronx and Shanique are flying to Miami tomorrow. Shanique will visit her music-producer boyfriend named Hector, and Bronx is making a guest appearance on a reality show. Summer and Ben are taking a drive up to Vermont. They plan to work on baby number one. And Claire has a date with a man whose name she's not ready to reveal.

"What about you, Treasure?" Shanique asks. "Fucking the day away with that sexy fiancé of yours?"

I stop myself from scoffing. Instead, I maintain an expert poker face when I say, "Dinner with the fam."

There's a collection of gasps, then they all playfully bow their heads in prayer and say, "Amen."

I chuckle. They're all aware of the sort of drama that's sure to arise when the Groves get together.

CRAVING THE MOMENT I CAN TRY OUT MY NEW bed, which looks extraordinarily comfortable, I walk slowly to the dining room to clear the table. When I make it back, my jaw drops as I lock eyes with Achilles. Then my eyes track down to the plates he's holding, one in each hand.

The way he's frowning is a telltale sign that he's not in a good mood. And I think I know why.

"Okay," I say with a deflated sigh. "I'm sorry for inviting guests without telling you first. Caroline said you wanted me to make myself at home." I end with a conciliatory shrug. I mean, my get-together with friends should be no big deal. It's not like he came home to me in the throes of a full-fledged party.

He still doesn't say anything, and the grumpy look on his face doesn't change either. "And I'll clean up," I say, raising my eyebrows at the plates he's holding.

"This table and these chairs are not to be used." His voice is merely a whisper, but it's strong and forceful.

I jerk my head back as a defiant wave of energy surges through me. "But I don't understand. It's a table. These are chairs," I say, gripping the top of the chair I'm standing behind.

"They're made for people to sit on, and they're positioned around a dinner table. We eat food at a dinner table." What did I just say? I don't think what I said made any sense. *Oh, my spinning head and gurgling stomach.*

Achilles points to his right and says, "Use the dining room on the east side of the kitchen."

I shift my attention to the table that I actually spent a few minutes admiring when I first saw it. It has strips of solid wood and silver metal made to resemble the branches of sunbursts. It's a very quality piece of furniture, even if it's a little too masculine for my tastes, and it's clear to see that it's expensive too.

"But why do you even have a table like this if you don't want to use it properly? I mean, are you so hell-bent on being a miserable prick?"

He looks confused by what I just said. I'm certainly confused by what I just said. It's a large leap from asking about his table to calling him a prick. I mean, my aunt Heartly has artifacts and furniture all over her house that she doesn't want anyone to touch. I've never called her a prick because of it. But Achilles is not Heart. No… he's something else to me, and that something else that I cannot name at the moment is why I'm so infu-

137

riated by him telling me to steer clear of his precious dining room set.

"Just do as I ask," he says with a strangely even voice. "And the cleaners will arrive shortly."

A wave of dizziness passes through my head, and when I blink, my eyelids almost get stuck closed. The truth is, I simply don't have the energy to argue with someone who plays it the way he does. He actually reminds me of Max. They have a lot in common. No wonder they hate each other. It's as if Achilles is no longer in the room as my thoughts begin to wander. Frankly, all I want to do right now is go to bed.

"This table is specially made," he continues. I detect a little desperation in his voice. It's as if he wants me to understand why he's being so fussy about his table.

"Specially made for what?" I ask in a biting tone. "To sit in front of the window? To catch light and degrade over time until one day you'll have to replace it again? Why have it if you're not going to enjoy it?" Because you're such a joyless person, I want to scream. My heart is beating like crazy and my body shaking. I've whipped myself up into a frenzy.

After a moment of glaring at me as if he

heard everything I just said in gibberish, his ruffled eyebrows even out. If I'm not mistaken, I think I saw his eyes dip down to my chest. The movement occurred so fast that I can't confirm it. "And the lighting," he says in an unperturbed voice. "Don't change it."

Wow. He's such a jerk. "I didn't touch your lighting. And sorry for believing that you wanted me to make myself at home in your overpriced penthouse. I forgot that hospitality isn't your style."

He says nothing, only grimaces, which is also a Max kind of response in the face of frantic energy. My tactic is all wrong, and I'm still too exhausted to correct it. And he stands tall, his wide muscular chest as stalwart as a steel wall stares back at me. I should storm away from him, but my feet are firmly planted against the marble. Storming off is never my style. I always like to end a disagreement with some sort of recon-ciliation.

Achilles's lips twitch like he wants to say some-thing but is thinking better about it. The doorbell rings, and he looks up and calls for Lara, who answers back that she's ready to clean. Of course he would summon the cleaning crew. I'm pretty sure the cleaning job I did in the kitchen isn't up to his standards.

I'm done. I can no longer engage in this moment. I spin on my heels and let my feet carry me away from Achilles Lord. Fuming, I storm off, visualizing my suitcase. It's in my closet. I handed it off to the bellman upon arrival, and at the conclusion of my guided tour with Caroline, I found my suitcase sitting empty in my closet. I'm still not sure how I feel about people I've never seen or spoken to touching my things. That's another problem with this damn penthouse—it's too high-end. I should sneak out of this place in the middle of the night. I'd go to my apartment, which is preferably closer to the ground. Maybe, when I finally shake my stress cold, I'll call Alex Shaw, invite him to a hotel suite, and let him fuck Achilles out of my system.

Oh no, is Achilles in my system?

My sigh originates deep from my gut as I finish climbing the stairway and plod to the sanctuary of a bedroom that Achilles has prepared for me.

"Damn it," I mutter.

Alex Shaw is off limits. Sleeping with him, trusting him to keep our involvement secret, is a big risk. Plus, Lynx will kill me if he finds out I'm screwing around with one of his players.

I sink down on the foot of the bed. I should still leave, though. I should pack my suitcase and get the hell out of Dodge.

The Northeast Garden

≈

TREASURE GROVE

hat is that sound?

I open one eye, and that brings me closer to fully waking up. There it goes again. It's my cell phone. But my arms feel glued to the mattress, and my brain is foggy. Instead of opening the other eye, I close the one that was open.

"Dang it," I mumble as the classic ringtone erupts for the third time and then stops.

Last night after dinner, I didn't pack my suitcase and escape to my apartment. The adrenaline burst I got from being angry at Achilles only lasted so long. As soon as I stepped into my bedroom, the comfort of the space affected my mood. He really did do a fantastic job designing this space. Everything is so… right. The walls are the right color. The temperature is perfect. And the bed, *oh* the bed, it's the most comfortable thing I've ever slept on.

So I measured my aching head, scratchy throat, and lethargic limbs against my diminishing anger. That's when I stripped out of my clothes, brushed my teeth, washed off my makeup, and slid into bed.

At first, I couldn't fall asleep. The view of the bright sky burned my eyes. Then I saw the blackout blinds pinned to the top of the windows and located the lever attached to the bottom of the feature wall. I flipped the lever up, the blinds came down, and when it fell pitch black, just like it is now, I could finally get the shut-eye I needed.

My cell phone rings yet again, and this time, I make a valiant effort to swing my arm across my body to swipe my device off the bedside table. I groan as I roll onto my stomach because my head feels like a gong is knocking around inside it. And my body, forget about it. My joints and muscles feel as though I spent an hour in the gym struggling through a HIIT workout before going to bed.

The light from the screen of my cell phone

illuminates my face. My mom's name on the screen makes me struggle to sit up against the headboard.

I take note of the time before I answer. It's 6:54 p.m.

"Yikes," I breathe as anxiety, like flesh-eating fish, descends on me.

After a deep sigh filled with dread, I answer.

"Mom?" I say tiredly.

"Are you asleep?" Her loud voice is like a slap to my brain. She sounds appalled.

"If I were asleep, I wouldn't be answering your call." I hate being snippy with her, but because I feel so awful, my filter is broken.

"You're late. We left without you. I've been calling you for over an hour. If you hadn't answered this time, I was going to call Achilles to have him check on you. Unless you've left his condo?"

"No," I say with a sigh. Not yet.

"Okay, well, we're sending the helicopter back to collect you. Be at the landing pad by seven thirty."

She pauses, waiting for me to make the easiest response. I rub my throbbing temples. Maybe I have a head cold, because whatever's happening in my brain is causing enough discomfort to make me want to crawl back in bed and sleep some more.

"Mom, I'm not feeling so hot." I throw the warm covers off of me, and chills flutter across my skin as I plod to the bathroom and clutch the edge of the vanity as I try to breathe past a bout of nausea.

"Do you have the flu?" She sounds as if my condition irritates her.

"I'm just stress sick, I think."

"Okay, well, just come to dinner and tough it out, Treasure. Your grandmother insists that we all be there. It's important to her."

Now, how did I know she was going to say that? I don't think she's wrong. I've been toughing it out for ten years, and actually before then too. However, my mom is right. Tonight is about Grandmother. Plus, I want to see her so much and hug her. One big hug and all my stress will roll down the drain, and what's ailing me will magically disappear. That's the effect my grandmother has on me, on the world.

"Seven thirty, don't be late. Take two Tylenol. That should help," Londyn throws in for good measure.

I stand upright, winning that battle with nausea, and roll my eyes. "Seven thirty it is."

I DOWN TWO EXTRA-STRENGTH TYLENOL AND TWO vitamin C tablets and then wait for the moment the effects of both kick in. This is not going to be an easy night to get through. But I've already made up in my mind what I'll do. I'll hug Gran, make a plan to meet her for brunch or dinner next week, and then have the helicopter bring me back to the city. I can't stay. I can't eat. I'm not hungry.

I drag myself to my closet and put on my lime-green cardigan sweater dress. It's what I wear whenever I want to look presentable but feel comfortable. Suddenly, a wave of chills sizzles up and down my body.

This is stress sick, right?

Unfortunately, I've run out of time to figure out the answer. I free my loose curls from my pineapple ponytail, slide into my favorite pair of closed-toe Mary Jane sandals, grab my purse, and rush out of the room.

I have eight minutes and counting.

The penthouse is as quiet as a church at midnight. I don't think Achilles is home, and I'm not going to look for him either. But I walk light on my feet, just in case he's creeping through his own house.

My heart thumps like a broken radiator as I ride down in the elevator. Jeez, I feel like crap. I really should stay in bed. I feel so weak. But the elevator doors slide open, and I choose to keep toughing it out.

Three minutes left.

OKAY, SO I'M LATE. I RAN ALL THE WAY FROM Achilles's building to this one. Thankfully, it's only four blocks away and on the same street. I'm still trying to steady my breath as I dash out of the elevator and down the final hallway that opens to the rooftop helipad. The bustle of getting here took a lot out of me, and I'm sweating like a racehorse. Thankfully, the helicopter is waiting. I check the time on the face of my phone. I'm three minutes late, which I think is pretty good considering how I'm feeling.

I'm groggy when we lift off. I really do think I

hit rock bottom. I must be crazy, going through with dinner. I should know better than to push myself this way. But at least I'm putting more distance between me and Achilles.

My sigh of dread spills out of my nostrils. That's right—I kissed him last night. I had forgotten all about what I had done until this very moment. What am I going to do about that? I have to explain to Achilles in depth why I did it. Maybe I owe him an apology for infringing on his personal space. Just because he's a man doesn't mean I get to kiss him without permission.

We're in midair, and all of my crappy symptoms rear their ugly heads—nausea, headache, chills, and exhaustion. But it doesn't matter. At least I've put enough miles between me and my new roommate, even if there's a conversation we must eventually have. I don't like the way we ended things last night. I have to fix it. Maybe we can talk tomorrow, or Tuesday.

I close my eyes, rest my head on the headrest, and whisper, "Wednesday." Ambient noise starts to lull me to sleep. "No, Thursday."

"Miss Grove, we've arrived," Jim, the pilot, says.

My eyelids stick as I try to separate the top from the bottom. After another attempt, I succeed. Jim is positioned in the doorway, watching me with a friendly and patient smile.

I want to smile back, but I wince instead as I sit up from leaning against the window. Every part of me aches. And goodness, I must've been really out of it. I didn't even hear or feel the helicopter land. Granted, the helicopter is silent. My parents shopped until they found one with the highest degree of safety, comfort, and noise-reduction. They certainly succeeded with this one.

"Thanks for the smooth landing," I say, mustering a wry lift to one side of my mouth.

His warm chuckle lets me know he appreciates my joke. Then he helps me out, and I notice something very interesting. All five helipad spaces in the lawn are occupied. So maybe Pais and Hercules did make it after all. The thought of Paisley being here makes me feel much stronger as I head to the house.

Heart and Xan's Greenwich, Connecticut, estate was once an enormous Victorian mansion owned by an extremely wealthy old-money family.

I can't recall which, though. However, Xan and Heart demolished that old house, much to the chagrin of their neighbors and the historical society, and built a home in its place that has lots of white stone and clear glass with the overall structure shaped like building blocks. The abode is modern contemporary to the extreme. It's a smart home too, equipped with all kinds of state-of-the-art automated functionalities.

I stop to check the time on my cell phone before getting too close to the double doors, brass with centered slices of frosted glass. When I make it to the middle section of the stacked cement steps, which lead from the lawn, the doors will automatically swing open in a dramatic fashion.

It's 8:31 p.m. My family should all be seated around the table. But before I go inside, I need to center myself. Also, my stomach feels heavy, and my nausea has returned with a vengeance. I sigh every ounce of breath out of my lungs and then think that it's not too late to turn around and ask Jim to fly me back to the city. Then, on an intake of tepid and slightly humid night air, I think that I need a moment to recuperate before facing my family.

I turn to my left and peer across the brilliantly

green grass. Whenever I sleep over at the estate, I stay in the room that lets me walk out and into a gorgeous Japanese garden with a koi pond with computer-generated fish swimming through it. The space is so surreal. Heart used the Japanese Garden at the Huntington Museum in California as her source of inspiration. The problem with using that restorative garden to clear my head and recover some strength is that it's too close to the dining room.

I look to my right. The Northeast Garden is in that direction. It's also beautiful and has a more relaxing feel. But the fireflies are the best part. Watching those insects light up an evening never gets old. Plus, that garden is far away from the main event, so I won't risk running into anyone. I trot across the lawn. Healthy grass squishes under the soles of my sandals.

My cell phone rings. Still moving and not slowing my pace because I don't want to be seen, I grimace at the screen.

"Shit," I mutter, already feeling something is wrong. "Hey, Lolly, what's going on?" My tone is rushed and business sharp.

"Are you running?" she asks.

"Yes."

"Okay. I hear it in your voice. I'll get right to it. The numbers suck, again."

I groan as I sigh but don't stop moving. "But how?"

Lolly begins listing each exorbitant expense, comparing the numbers from last month's expense report to the previous three months. Utilities, salaries, food costs, equipment, and so forth all lend to increasing my bottom line. At this pace, I'll never make enough money to pay back the trust.

Finally, I walk past two tall privacy hedges and then through a short labyrinth that leads into the garden. A strange scent is in the air, one that I never smell on Heart and Xan's property.

"Treas, are you still with me?" Lolly asks.

I whip my face toward a sound of someone breathing and that feeling one gets when there's another person in the vicinity.

Then, suddenly, I'm locking eyes with the last person in the world I thought I would see tonight at this house.

"Treasure?" Lolly sounds worried.

"I'm here," I'm only barely able to say. "Um, let's talk tomorrow. I have to go." Without waiting

153

for her response, I end our call with my head feeling cloudy.

My mouth is caught open, and my attention is trapped by Achilles Lord's gaze.

———

In the middle of the opened pergola that runs up against the house stands Achilles Lord. The lights woven into the many flowers and trimmed bushes illuminate him as though he were a famous male model posing during a photoshoot. Quickly, I see that he's wearing black pants that his fit thighs and strong legs were specially made for him. He's not wearing a crisp white dress shirt, which is the sort of garment I thought he slept in —heck, he'd be buried in. Instead, he's wearing a light-gray polo shirt that appears to be made of the softest cotton material. I hate that he looks so attractive—I really do.

Then I notice the cigarette caught between his lips as he's frozen in place just like I am.

"Hello?" I say carefully.

His stare seems to open up and spread across my face. "Hello." He sounds just as chilly as always.

I swallow to moisten my tight and achy throat. "What are you doing here?"

Cigarette captured between his teeth, he scoffs as if the answer to my question is too incredible to speak. He takes the cigarette out of his mouth.

"You smoke?" I ask unthinkingly. Not many people smoke anymore.

"No," he says, and I think I see a suggestion of a smile.

"Then why are you smoking?" The words leave my mouth unfiltered. But yeah… I'd like to know why he's smoking if he doesn't smoke.

"I quit," he says, face deadpan.

I point at the cigarette between his fingers, and smoke streaks from the tip. "Well, that's exactly what quitting looks like."

To my surprise, he blurts a light chuckle. It feels like the iceberg between us is slowly starting to melt.

Anxiously, I check over my shoulder. There's no turning back now, and it's not as if I want to. The big question hasn't been answered yet either. So I finish closing the distance between us. "Are you here on business?"

Achilles's infamous grimace is back with a vengeance. "You don't know?"

Now I frown too. "I don't know what?"

"Why I've been invited to dinner? Hell, I think it's why you've been invited too."

I visualize the dining room, where I should be in my assigned seat by now. My mom is probably continuously checking her watch. Pretty soon, she's going to excuse herself to call me.

"I'm having dinner with my family. My grand-mother is in town and—"

I'm cut off by his bitter laugh, which stops when he drags on his cigarette. It's as if what I said has triggered him into needing a puff.

I lean sideways to see past him to the glass sunroom and its French doors which open to the entrance of the garden from a step-down foyer. When my eyes meet Achilles's again, he's already staring at me. No, it's more than a stare, his eyes are exploring me. And the depth with which they're doing so momentarily takes my breath away.

"Your grandmother and my grandfather arranged this get-together," he says as he smashes the tip of his cigarette with the sole of his expen-sive leather shoes.

What he said isn't computing in my head. It makes no sense. What do his grandfather and my grandmother have in common? "I don't understand."

"They're in a relationship, which has been going on for many years."

My jaw drops, and I am speechless. My grandmother and Achilles's grandfather, who happens to be my grandfather's nemesis, getting it on?

Now it all makes so much sense, and because of it, I burp a laugh. "Am I surprised? No," I say with another laugh. "It's even better than Shakespearian drama. It's a low-rated soap opera."

I grin at my own joke. I mean, that was funny, but he's frowning at me again.

"Why do you look at me that way?" I blurt.

He's still doing it when he asks, "Look at you in what way?"

"Like you're going to take an axe to my head. I mean, should I be worried?"

His frown intensifies. "Worried about what?"

I shrug. "I don't know. I mean, you keep a writing pen in a fish tank, and you display body parts around your house."

I didn't know his frown could turn more severe than it already was, but it does somehow.

His lips part as if he wants to address what I said but can't find the words.

I close my eyes to shake my head. What's wrong with me? I pretty much called him a weirdo to his face. I squish my facial features together as more embarrassment blushes through me. "I'm sorry. And I'm also sorry about that kiss."

Thankfully, his expression changes. The frown is gone, but he's still staring at me as if he's lost for words.

Finally, he clears his throat and says, "It's okay. The kiss. I know why you did it."

My eyebrows flash up. "You do?" I ask in a high-pitched tone.

"You were proving to your friends that we're a real couple." He looks at the smashed tip of his cigarette like he wishes he hadn't ended its life. "It seems we have a huge problem convincing others that we're together."

I grunt facetiously as I mutter, "I wonder why?"

His head flicks slightly to one side. He's thinking something about me. "I'm sorry for calling you a debutante. I don't remember saying it, but if you do, then I'm sorry. You're obviously not a debutante."

That's interesting. "Obviously?" My curious tone begs him to elaborate.

Finally, I get a real, robust grin out of Achilles Lord. "You're…" he starts but then swallows.

Very quickly, his smile fades, and I wait for him to finish whatever he was going to say as kinetic energy swirls around us, lassoing us together.

"There's someone we should talk to… a therapist," he says, sounding strained.

"Talk to a therapist about what?"

"Us—doing a better job presenting as a couple. We have to make it believable." His pause hangs. "If it's going to work."

I can't take my eyes off his lips. They're mesmerizing. They felt so soft against mine. Our kiss was as light as air. It was so sensual, easy, natural.

Oh no… I turn my head. Attraction forces me to look away from him and set my focus solely on the garden. It's an English garden, and the fireflies are kindling around the flowers and the tall grasses. They're always so happy around the peonies and dahlias. They also love hovering above the tranquil pond which is encircled by more flowers.

"Fireflies," Achilles says.

I take a glance at him and then back at the pond. I love that his gaze has followed mine. Watching fireflies glow is steadily quelling the desire in my body. As usual, they've stolen my attention. I miss them. "Yeah," I say with a sigh.

Loud chiming erupts, forcing me to look at the face of my cell phone. It's my mom. I knew she'd call sooner rather than later. I have to go inside, but still, there's something about this moment Achilles and I are sharing that's signaling some sort of change. Being in his presence is finally easy, but then, it's more than that. It's as if standing next to him, watching the fireflies in silence, is something I could do all night long.

Families Dinner

Achilles stayed behind. He said he needed to make a phone call. But I think he wanted space to reset after the strange and stimulating moment we shared. My head felt like it was dancing in the clouds when I made it to the dining room, hugged my grandmother, and kissed my parents, then Xan and Heartly, and then my brother. Max doesn't do hugs, but he and the storm cloud that he rode in on are present too. However, Achilles isn't the only surprise guest. The older gentleman sitting next to my grandmother must be his grandfather. I don't know his name, but Paisley does. He's very handsome. If he's any indication of how well the Lord brothers will age, then they have a lot to look forward to.

Then there's a woman, who certainly is the Lord brothers' mother. I remember her name is Marigold. She's close to my parents' age and is pretty, having a regal quality that people who have known no other lifestyle but money and privilege have. She's already appraising me when I look at her. It's as if she's trying to see if I'm good enough for her favorite son or something.

As far as the mood, it's odd. It feels like a shaky ceasefire hangs in the air. My grandmother and Achilles's grandfather appear too syrupy. My dad looks as if he's about to have a conniption. Xan has that faraway look in his eyes, as if he'd rather be anywhere else but here. My brother and Max are barely in their seats. I have a feeling they're going to flee this scene at any moment. And then there's Orion—he's staring at me as if he's a werewolf and I'm a fresh piece of meat. Although I missed the big announcement, I'm certain that Orion could give a damn about it. He likes to keep himself unburdened by commitment, work, and I'm certain family affairs too.

"Honey, find your seat," my grandmother says.

As she lifts herself slightly out of her chair, my grandmother's finger guides me to a place setting marked by a card with my name written in pressed gold cursive letters. A lot of time and attention went into setting the tables. Gold is the theme of the night. The dinner, dessert, and bread plates are designed with ivory and gold stripes. The leaf doilies under the dinnerware are golden too. The design aesthetic is so different than usual. I have no doubt that Grandmother was in charge of tonight's fluff show. She must've really wanted to affect the mood in the right way. Yet despite all the beauty around us, no one is glowing gold.

"Treasure Chest," my grandmother says, "this is my husband, Hugo."

Ohh… my jaw suddenly becomes unhinged. Achilles never said anything about the two of them being married.

"What?" my dad's voice erupts. "You're married?"

Ohh… she hadn't mentioned it until now.

Grandmother looks at her husband with wide eyes that say, "Oh no, honey, I screwed up."

I count one, two, now three seconds of silence, which are the calm before the storm. However, all of a sudden, I feel dizzy. I'm certain the adrenaline spike I experienced from my encounter with

163

Achilles has worn off. My stomach is queasy and my head tight.

Two servers roll in tonight's entrée on a silver cart. I've already gleaned from the plate beside mine that it's braised short ribs with red wine sauce with a corn-and-roasted-carrot-type hash. The smell exacerbates my nausea.

"Well…" Grandmother's husband starts. "Yes. We are married, but…"

Then, Leo starts laughing. It's a laugh that begins slow and deep, originating deep in his body, perhaps in a place where old wounds bleed. The sound is so maniacal that he's gaining the attention of everyone at the table. Even Orion stops making eyes at me to see if my father hasn't morphed into an imp.

My mom and I lock eyes. She appears just as worried as I am as she clings to his shoulder and rubs the upper part of his back to support and calm him. That's when I notice he's wearing a light-blue dress shirt. It's his favorite color. I think he was looking forward to tonight's dinner until grandmother's news ruined it for him.

"Babe, it's okay," Mom says consolingly. All the blood has drained from her face too.

"So this is it?" My dad laughs. "We're fucking

here because the two of you…" His pointed finger shifts between Leslie and Hugo. "Cheated on my dad."

"I'm just as upset about this as Xander is," Marigold says.

"Xander?" Heartly chirps. "You mean Leo." She zeroes in on my dad, looking at him with pure contempt. "My husband is Xander, and the one who's falling apart at the seams"—she points a lazy finger at my mother—"is her husband."

My mom scoffs as if Heartly's palm has just slapped her across the face. "Are you really going to make this about you and me?" My mom drops her elbows on the table, giving Heart a vicious look. "You know what? Since tonight is about the truth, let's hash this out. Why are you always needling me? What is it? Are you jealous of me?"

Heart lifts her perfectly manicured eyebrows as high up as they can go, but she doesn't say a thing. She's not one to lose her cool after casting the first stone. But her reaction is a tactic more than a demonstration of collectedness. And this response of hers always drives my mom crazy.

Unfortunately, Paisley isn't here, but after being caught in the middle of our mothers' sense-less squabbles, Paisley and I made a pact to stay out of the middle of them. That pact stands even if one of us isn't in the room. In the early days, my mom seemed shocked that she couldn't rile me up about the shit Heart supposedly did or said to her. But over the years, she finally understands, and I think prefers, that her battles with my aunt are her own.

Lowering her eyebrows, Heart tilts her chin slightly and then glares death beams at my mom. "No. I am not jealous of you, Londyn." Heart's voice is as steady as her shoulders.

My mom jabs a finger against the tablecloth. "Then stop taking digs at me."

"I wasn't taking a dig at you. I took one at your husband. For Christ's sake, Leo, you're not a little boy…"

"Enough, Heart," Xander blares, watching my dad with his own brows knitted in concern.

My uncle's booming voice is just what the table needed to restore silence and that same mood I walked into when I first entered the dining room.

But still, none of them notice that I am not doing so well. I want to ask if someone can turn down the air-conditioning. I'm so cold.

"Leo's not wrong, Mother," Xan says. "You did this all wrong."

And oh, my aching head.

"Frankly, I don't think we should be dining together since we have a hearing on Tuesday," Max announces as he tosses his cloth napkin on top of his plate.

That one act from Max and noticing the untouched plate of food in front of the chair next to me makes me clutch my stomach. Is Achilles sitting next to me?

Someone else is laughing in pure amusement, and it's my brother. "Grandmother." His chair screeches against the wood as he scoots it back. He's suddenly on his feet and is soon kissing our grandmother on the temple. "I came for your announcement. Congratulations, I wish you the best, but I have a team meeting to get back to."

If the air wasn't already jam-packed with tension, I'd call bullshit on Lynx's team meeting. This is the start of Lynx and Max's customary escape. They will leave, one after the other, and then head back to the city, where they'll hang out in one of many high-end private clubs. I'm on the verge of calling bullshit on them anyway since I feel so much like crap, and why not join in the general spirit of the night? But Achilles walking—no, floating—into the dining room steals my full attention.

As Achilles takes his seat beside me, Max, right on cue, says, "I'm leaving too."

Like Lynx, he kisses Grandmother goodbye while ignoring Hugo. "I'll call you tomorrow, Dad," he says, and then he's out of the room before Grandmother can object. Normally, she would try to guilt him into staying. But I think tonight, Grandmother is taking Max's congratulations and him not blowing up like Leo had as a win.

"Are you okay?" Achilles asks.

I stop rubbing my aching temples to look at him. "What?" I ask, barely able to keep my eyes open. I'm going downhill fast. Funny, Achilles seems to be the only one who notices my demise.

"Treasure, I want to talk to you," Orion whispers.

I'm shaking my head before the words "go to hell" can blurt out of my mouth.

"Hugo, exactly how long have you been…" I catch my dad glancing at me, as if my presence is making him reconsider what he's going to ask.

"How long have you been in a relationship with my mother?"

I don't even mask my impatient grunt. I feel as if I should say something to make this night advance faster. I don't know how much longer I can sit in this chair.

"Well, it's not like Grandmother and Grandfather had an award-winning relationship, Dad," I say, surprising even myself.

Leo flicks his attention on me. But there's an unfocused look in his eyes. It's as though his despair hadn't allowed him to absorb a word I just said.

"She has a point," I'm so thankful to hear Heart say. "Charles and Leslie never lived with each other. I know I never fooled myself into believing they actually loved each other."

"But Charles and I did love each other," Grandmother interjects. "In our own way, we did. It wasn't romantic love. It was…" A solemn mask falls over Grandmother's face.

The silence waits to be absorbed by whatever Grandmother will say, but she doesn't say anything.

"How about we get through this dinner for the sake of…" Heart's words stop cold turkey.

I, on the other hand, gradually swallow another bout of nausea. I swear I can't do this for another five minutes. I'll have to excuse myself shortly.

"Family," Hugo says to cover the silence. "For the sake of our families getting along for once."

Now it's Xan who lets out an uncustomary scoff. "If you want our families to get along, then call off your hounds. Let TRANSPOT go."

Hugo holds his hands out with his palms facing Xan. "I'm not linked to the business anymore."

"Is that your cop-out?" Xan retorts.

"Hey! Watch how you speak to my grandfather, Xander," Achilles blares.

Oh gosh. I don't want to love how he stepped in to defend his grandfather's honor, but I do. Orion didn't say a word. Just like I knew he wouldn't, because he only thinks about himself—no, his cock—he only thinks about his cock, first and last.

"I was thinking, ladies," Grandmother says as her eyes shift from my mom's face to Heart's and then to Marigold's. "How about we do something together?"

Grandmother mentions a collaborative

fundraiser between the Grove Philanthropic Foundation and the Lord Charitable Foundation. At least the women have picked up their eating utensils and have started to dig into tonight's dinner before it gets too cold. I think they like the sound of throwing a charity event together. My mom and Heart live for them. It's the only time when they actually come together and behave like real sisters-in-law.

"I like it," Londyn says. "Marigold, I would love to finally work in conjunction with TLCO. You all do tremendous work."

"Mother, how long?" Leo's angry roar seems to rise from the grave to haunt the room.

But it's not my dad's angry voice that sends chills up and down my skin. And whatever I have left in my stomach is in my throat, especially now that a server has placed a plate of piping-hot, fragrant food in front of me.

"Treasure?" Achilles whispers, his voice full of concern.

"No," I groan. "I'm not feeling well." My eyes are closed, and I'm concentrating extremely hard on keeping the little I have in my stomach from going blah all over the twin short ribs on my plate.

Then my dad announces that maybe we

should leave since I don't look so well. Finally, he's noticed.

"But honey, we haven't even started the third course." I can hear in my mom's voice that she doesn't want to go anymore at all. They've started talking about charity events, and hell will freeze over before she lets Heart, Leslie, and Marigold continue the discussion without her.

"Xan and Heart have a room for Treasure. The one with the koi pond," my mom says.

"Sure, Treasure's room is right around the corner," Heart tacks on. "She can sleep here tonight. And we'll do coffee and girl talk in the morning." I can't see her face, but I'm sure she's smiling at me as if I'm going to magically feel like having a coffee-laden tea party with her when I wake up.

Plus, tomorrow is Monday. Heartly's never home during the week. There's no way she's going to stay home with sick old me.

"No," Achilles says with a tone that's hard to debate with. "I'll take her home to sleep in her own bed."

The silence that follows is full of shame about what we've all agreed to do for money. I mean, even Grandmother and Hugo are in on it. I know this because she thought to sit me beside Achilles, in fact, presenting us as a couple.

"Achilles, you should also stay as we discuss the charity event," Marigold says. When he turns to his mother, she raises her eyebrows.

"Orion will stay."

Oh no…

"No, you stay. I'll take her home," Orion retorts.

Oh no… I take short breaths, trying to hold down what wants to rise higher up my throat as my gag reflex kicks in.

"What the hell is wrong with you? Stay in your seat," Achilles blares. He's already standing. "Do something for our family for once instead of the other way around."

He asks if I can stand on my own. But it's too late to stop myself now. It happens. I vomit all over the food on my plate, Grandma's fine china, and the silky ivory tablecloth.

Getting Well Soon

TREASURE GROVE

T he night's humid air laced with a touch of a cool breeze rubs my face. I was so embarrassed when I threw up all over my dinner. I should've gotten up and run to the toilet. Who am I kidding, though? I would've never made it. What happened was inevitable.

After I threw up, my mom raced over to put her arms around me. I heard a lot of commotion. Someone wiped my mouth. Achilles insisted he take me home and mentioned a doctor. My entire family was wholeheartedly on board with my going home with him after he said that. Even if I could have objected, I wouldn't. There was something settling about the thought of sleeping in the same bed that I slept in last night. It was very comfortable. I want more of it.

I can hardly put one heavy foot in front of the other as I move at a snail's pace. I'm weak, cold even in the warm night, and achy, but at least I don't want to throw up anymore. And Achilles helps me with each step. I'm grateful that he's patient with me. I would stay far away from his strong body, sublime scent that doesn't make my stomach turn, and the connective energy pouring from his body if I felt better. Because sure, he's helping now, but when I'm feeling fine and back on my feet, how nice will he be then? I would shrug him off in the name of self-preservation, but I can't. I need his help.

We've advanced down a cement walk that leads to the helipad field. I try to muster up enough strength to walk up the three short steps into the helicopter, but I couldn't have done it without a lift from Achilles. He's so strong.

"Hang in there," he says as he leans his upper body across me to strap on my seat belt.

He's so close.

"Why are you being so nice to me?" I mumble. I ask because I feel like this is a trick.

My eyelids flicker closed. I can no longer see

his face, but I know he's scowling as if he's confused.

The engine smoothly purrs into action. Second by second, I'm getting more comfortable and closer to falling asleep. He says something, though. He's asking me a question. I can tell it's a question by the intonation of his voice, only I don't know what he said. I would have to ask him to say it again, but I can't.

I can't.

* * *

Achilles grabs me by one wrist and Orion by the other. They're tugging me like I'm a rope, each man offering many a grimace, hiss, and roar like he's determined to rip me out of his brother's grasp. However, I'm in the middle, watching them, unable to feel my limbs stretch like taffy.

I fix my eyes on Orion. Now that I'm getting a long and steady look at him, he's not working as hard as Achilles. He's looking at me with those eyes I detest. They're laughing, unserious, you-can-never-depend-on-me eyes. They're also I-want-to-devour-you, lay-you-down-and-give-you-more-orgasms-than-your-body-can-handle eyes. They're eyes that scream, *I want to love you, I want you to fall in love with me, and then I'll get some kind of sick charge from breaking your heart. And I'll break your heart. Then I'll come back into your life. I'll convince you that you read the circumstances of our split all wrong. I'll kiss you. Make love to you. And then betray you yet again.*

That's when I snatch my wrist out of Orion's grasp, and he easily loses his grip.

* * *

I think I get up to pee.

There are people around me.

Oh, I ache.

I'm so sleepy.

I think it's Caroline who helps me to the toilet.

"Drink this…" Achilles says.

Yuck. What is that?

Umm… I feel a lot better, though.

* * *

I'm facing Achilles. He's taller than I am by a good eight inches. I'm forced to tilt my head back to look him in the eyes. What a sexy man he is. What deep, dark, and hypnotic eyes he has. The backs of his enormous fingers trail down one side of my face until they delicately caress my chin, and his thumb slides across my lower lip. I can't move a muscle.

"I hate you," Achilles whispers.

The words I want to speak struggle to make it

past my lips. But I push, grimacing, fighting to finally say, "But why?"

My eyes pop open.

* * *

I'm in bed surrounded by comfy bed linens and fluffy pillows. The blinds are up. Sunlight filters in through the enormous windows. The view isn't so unsettling from my bed which is far back from the glass. I'm still not one hundred percent back in my body, though. But I twist, stretching like a cat waking from a nap. No aches or pains. I feel good—really good.

What happened last night?

Droplets of memory drip into my brain as if from a leaky faucet. I was on the helicopter. Achilles strapped me into my seat. He said...

What did he say?

Damn it, I can't remember.

Then I fell asleep. I sort of remember him cradling me and my arms wrapped around his neck and my lips near the side of his face. I wanted to kiss him. I had an overwhelming desire to do it. I was thankful I could sleep while he carried me, though. Being awake felt arduous. I trusted him.

There was a woman. I think it was Caroline. I

push the covers down to look at myself. I'm wearing my pink-and-white striped satin pajamas. I'm not in my lime-green sweater dress, which I would've totally worn to bed if it were left up to me.

I'm starving.

I kick the covers off my legs and carefully sit up against the headboard. Yep, my body feels rejuvenated.

On the nightstand sits a nearly empty plastic bottle of electrolytes. Now I remember Achilles insisting that I drink most of the contents. I gasp. He was in my room, and a doctor wearing a white coat told me to open my mouth, and then I held a thermometer under my tongue.

Oh no…

At some point, and maybe a few times, I went to the bathroom and fell asleep on the toilet. I cover my face and wait for the embarrassment to pass.

My stomach growls like a ravenous wolf.

I'm hungry, very hungry.

It's time to eat.

* * *

My bathroom smells fresh and lemony. It has been cleaned recently. While brushing my teeth, I check my face in the mirror. When did I take my makeup off? I don't remember doing it. I remember wanting to do it, though.

I finish brushing my teeth and then twist and tie my hair up high on my head. But something feels insufficient about the way I'm presenting right now. I'm staring in the mirror at the single Treasure Grove, who lives all by herself, and certainly not with Achilles Lord.

I exhale slowly and let the back of my fingers trail down my cheek and stop at my chin. My skin flushes as I feel a sense of déjà vu. But it wasn't me who touched myself this way. I feel as if Achilles trailed the backs of his fingers down the side of my face, cupped my chin, and then whispered something to me.

"Hmm," I moan, lost in the image of myself staring back at me in the mirror.

Maybe that never happened at all. And after one deep inhale and long exhale, I'm back in the moment and anxious to start my day.

Judging by the bright quality of light flowing into my bedroom, I'd say it's late Monday morning. I'm certain Achilles isn't home. He's a workaholic, thank God. But still, I let my hair live free from the topknot. All men like wild bedhead.

Instead of my grimy pajamas, I put on a yellow tank dress. I'm fine with the material hugging all my round parts. I'm also fine with my nipples pushing against the material. I turn to get a look of my rear end in the standing mirror. My eyebrows flash up. "Nice," I whisper, hyping myself up. I can now head downstairs.

My day builds out in my head as I walk to the kitchen. I recall my last conversation with Lolly. The bills are mounting yet again. No matter what, I can't stop myself from overspending on that restaurant of mine.

Before taking the stairs down to the first floor, I stop and turn in the direction of Achilles's bedroom. I should thank him for taking such good care of me. It had been a tough haul, but he helped me get through.

But I would never show up at his bedroom door without permission, especially wearing this lounge dress. I see our kiss from Saturday night and him staring at me in the garden.

"Oh shit," I say, looking down at my pebbling nipples.

Then I rush back to my bedroom and put on a nice fresh pair of baggy pajamas.

* * *

My eyes swell wide as I gasp when I see the time and date on the oven's clock. It's Tuesday, not Monday, and it's 10:03 a.m. I squandered a full day being sick. Damn it.

I bet the voicemail on my cell phone is full. I know I have hundreds of emails to respond to, and meetings—I missed all of Monday's meetings. I tug the refrigerator door open and take out a carton of eggs. There's no time to screw around. I have to cook myself a vegetable omelet, dash upstairs to get dressed and call Lolly, and then take a cab to the restaurant.

I freeze with my fingers curved around a fresh block of American cheese. *Where's my cellphone, anyway?* I work faster, dicing up scallions, broccoli, and red, orange, and yellow bell peppers. I cook a strip of bacon for extra flavor.

"Good morning," Achilles says.

Squatting while searching through a lower cabinet for a cheese grater, I shoot up to my feet.

"Good morning," I squeak out. Seeing him has caught me off guard. "I can't find the cheese grater."

I'm mesmerized by Achilles's maleness as he walks in my direction. I recall the first time I saw him walk into Grove Family Bank building. He wasn't just strutting for public consumption. It's his normal gait. He is a man with the utmost confidence and natural regality. His eyes are on me, assessing as he approaches. He looks so yummy in a flawless black suit with a crisp white shirt beneath. "You look better," he says as he opens the cabinet next to the oven and takes out the cheese grater.

"I feel better," I say in a low voice and then swallow to rid myself of this rush of lust I'm experiencing. He's so tall and athletic. I bet he's strong in bed.

"You had a case of viral gastroenteritis," he says.

I snap out of my stupor and take the grater from him. For those few seconds that we are holding the grater together, a flash of electric energy passes through me.

I start grating the cheese as my mind flashes back to the dinner from hell at Heart and Xan's house. I cringe, remembering how he saw me vomit on my plate. "So, any word on how dinner ended the other night?" I ask.

I turn in time to see Achilles lower the fire under the pan I'm cooking bacon in.

"Shoot," I say, shaking my head. I almost

burnt the bacon. Having him around while I'm cooking is knocking me off my game.

"They didn't kill each other," he says, pushing the button to automatically make coffee. "Want one?"

He means coffee. I nod. "Thanks."

"You're welcome."

We smile at each other, and I love the lightness between us for once. And gosh, he smells so good. His scent reminds me of a brand-new day fresh with possibilities.

I start grating again. "Was Caroline around?"

"Yes, she dressed you and prepared you for bed, and helped in other ways."

I sigh with relief. Without my asking, Achilles picks up the tongs and flips over the bacon sizzling in the pan.

"So, why are you being so nice to me?" I ask.

"Are you not used to people being nice to you?" His tone is casual. Now he's wetting a dishcloth.

"Yes, but not you."

He's wiping the bacon grease off the spot where I laid the tongs.

"I was going to clean that," I say.

"I apologize for the other night. You didn't

know that I prefer that no one eat at the custom-made table. Caroline didn't know either."

"You want one?" I ask, pointing at the stack of cheese in front of me. I mean, I really don't want to get into a back-and-forth about his special table. This is his penthouse, not mine. On top of that, he's reminding me why it will never work between us. I believe the world is our oyster. Nothing is sacred. All has been created for us to enjoy. He believes in encapsulating and incarcerating objects. He's a worshipper. I'm not.

His eyebrows are still knitted, like he's considering his answer which is taking forever. "I can't," he finally says. "But we have a meeting this afternoon."

I frown. "We do?" I don't remember scheduling a meeting with Achilles on my calendar.

"Yes, with the relationship expert I mentioned the other night."

"What? Why?"

"Have you read *TRM* lately?" he asks and scowls as he looks off. "I gotta figure out how to buy that fucking magazine and then kill it."

I raise my eyebrows, actually liking the sound of that. Before this whole deal for the money, I would've wholeheartedly disagreed with him. But now, I think chopping off *TRM*'s head isn't such a bad idea.

I fold my arms over my chest. "And I'll help you."

Ah, a new expression appears on Achilles's face. He looks equally surprised and pleased by what I said. We smile at each other for way too long. It feels like we should kiss goodbye or maybe shake hands—basically, touch in one way or another. But instead, he nods sharply and says, "Enjoy your day."

"You too," I barely utter.

And then he turns, and I watch him gait away. So, so regal.

My sigh is feverish with lust. I can't... nope. He's off limits.

Top Rag Mag

YIKES! HE SAID SHE'S FAKING IT.

" Mega superstar Simon Linney has agreed to go on record with us.

Well, you know what that means?

First, let's get on with it, and then you can figure out what it means for yourself.

Simon Linney, who was recently punched repeatedly in the head by Orion Lord—at least that's what all of your videos show (and for it, I want to not kiss, but tongue whoever created the camera phone)—claims that Treasure Grove and Achilles Lord are indeed engaged in a fake relationship.

Linney suspects their union is the result of a business deal.

Of course, we must say that his claims are alleged. However, he's not the only bird who's singing about the couple's perplexing relationship. We have proof that the groom-to-be's distant cousin, Victoria Lord, has filed a fraud claim against the couple's relationship. The details of the claim are sealed—for now. Don't worry, we'll tell you more when we know more, and we will definitely know more.

However, this afternoon, in one of our famous staff meetings, one of your favorite writers asked a valid question: Why aren't the two ever seen in public together? No dates at Treasures. No making out on park benches like her cousin and his brother.

Maybe Simon Linney and Victoria Lord are onto something.

From the outside looking in, Achilles Lord and Treasure Grove's relationship is definitely a fraud. What do you think? Comment below.

The Session

TREASURE GROVE

Achilles has texted me the time our session with the counselor begins but not the address. He said he'll send a car to pick me up at five thirty and drive me to the location.

But I called him, and he answered on the first ring. "Just give me the address," I said rather snappishly.

"No. It's supposed to rain, and I'm going into a meeting. I'll see you later," he said and then ended our call.

I held my cell phone in front of my face and shouted, "Jerk!"

My door was open, so Lolly showed up in my

doorway and asked with surprise and intrigue, "Who were you talking to?"

I waved away an answer and said, "Nobody." I quickly stood. "We should get to our next meeting."

But Lolly handed me a large orange envelope and said, "This arrived for you."

What arrived was what I forgotten I had been waiting on—the script about how Achilles and I met. It was simple, and I wonder why I hadn't thought of it in the first place. We flew privately to Majorca to meet up with Hercules and Paisley one weekend last month. And I actually remember that weekend. It was the one weekend I stayed inside to comb over all the invoices so that I could get a better grasp on how I'd been spending. It seems as if tracking spending is a nonstop effort I partake in ever since opening my restaurant. Other than a few phone calls, I brunched or had dinner with no one. So there is no one to dispute the claim that I wasn't in Majorca on that particular Saturday or Sunday. Oh, the lies I've been telling for the money. They're building their own dark palace.

Anyway, the day has raced by so fast that there's too much to sort out. The meeting I'm in now began at five p.m. Lolly, Ingrid, our events manager, and I have been going down the list of celebrity parties that we'll be hosting this month. The celebrities' requests are expensive, and it seems each and every one of them wants us to accept the currency of their popularity rather than cold hard cash.

"It's so funny," Ingrid says, reading the list. "All the money they have, they forever want shit for free." She looks up to frown at me curiously. "Why is that? Are they that spoiled?"

"Yes," I say without delay. I know a lot of famous movie stars and music artists. Fame can go to the head faster than a speeding bullet.

Lolly sighs as her arms flop, and she drops the pages she's looking at onto the table. "So what do we do? Incur the cost ourselves?"

I've been around her long enough to know how loaded her question is. That look in her eyes is asking, do you want to pay to be popular or finally make some real money?

I gnaw on my bottom lip, confused about where the line is—the line between the value of being a hotspot for the Who's Who of the world or just being popular for making melt-in-your-mouth good food like the majority of the restaurants in New York City. Being a celebrity hot spot was my stab at standing out from the crowd.

I jump, startled when the alarm on my phone chimes. It's time I head out to meet the car that Achilles has waiting for me. I tell Lolly and Ingrid that I'll get back to them about the event expenses.

"But first, only write up an expense sheet that doesn't go over the amount of the money they're paying. Make sure you're as thrifty as possible." I rise to my feet seized by the overwhelming feeling that I don't have a second to spare. "Maybe that's our problem—giving them caviar when they only want to pay for tuna."

Lolly starts to say something, but I raise a finger and ask that she holds that thought until tomorrow morning.

"I have to go."

I OPEN MY LAPTOP AND CRUNCH MORE NUMBERS ON the way to my counseling session with Achilles. At this rate, I'll never be able to pay back the trust. And I can see it on Lolly's face. It seems we can't get a grip on our expenses. No matter what we try, they're out of hand. And what can we cut?

I slam my laptop shut and circle the tips of my fingers against my temples when the car rolls to a stop. I didn't pay attention to what neighborhood we're in. I duck my head to look for the nearest street sign—Third near Lexington. We're on the Upper East Side, and then Achilles walks out through the black-tinted glass door of the building we're in front of. Of course he's one of those people who's always either early or on time. I wish I had been well enough to sit through to the completion of Sunday night's dinner. I'm certain I would've gotten a more complete picture of the Lord family dynamic. Although, I do remember Achilles saying to Orion that he should remain at the table and be there for his family for once, or something to that effect. I bet Achilles is the responsible one who's always cleaning up Orion's fuckups.

I thank the driver, who opens my door, and as soon as I'm out and standing on the sidewalk, Achilles doesn't fail to give me that look. I don't know—maybe he's been a sourpuss for so long that he can't stop being one.

But he did smile this morning, and that's a good sign.

"Good afternoon," I say with a smile that's meant to be infectious.

He starts to speak but then seals his lips as he thinks better of it.

"Your reply should be 'Good afternoon,'" I say, helping him along.

"Good afternoon," he blurts and then glares at his watch. "We should get inside."

He moves to the door, which I can now see opens automatically. However, Achilles stands against the glass to make sure I enter before he does.

"Thank you," I say evenly, as if walking past him doesn't make my blood tickle my heart.

Then he places a large hand on the small of my back and says, "This way."

My knees nearly buckle from whatever powers of attraction he has over me. But I have to get a grip. I have to remind myself that I'm not one of those girls who fucks simply because she's attracted to a guy. *Personality makes you horny, Treas.* I keep telling myself that fib as we both cram ourselves into a tiny elevator.

We're quiet and both are watching the numbers on the panel above the door count up. I should say something to him.

"You look nice today," he says before I can speak.

I know I look nice today. I had him in mind when I slipped into a gold slinky midi dress that has a V-neckline that displays just enough cleavage to make him do a double take. I'm also wearing black patent-leather Mary Jane heels. I'm surprised he noticed, because his eyes haven't veered below my face, not once.

"Thank you," I say, still staring at the numbers. "Oh, and Majorca, huh?" I smile.

"I'm sure we had a ball," he says.

My eyebrows flash up as I cock my head to look at him in surprise. "Touché to Achilles Lord with a sense of humor." Then he frowns again. "I take that back."

Ding.

The elevator stops, and the doors slide open. Again, he stands against the frame to make sure I walk out before he does. This time, I don't say thank you, even though I want to. For some reason, I'm too embarrassed to say anything to him, and it makes no sense at all. He's the sourpuss who killed the mood, and now I'm embarrassed to say thank you? I can't make sense of it as I walk slightly behind him down a tight hallway with dark-green square-patterned carpet with little yellow flowers here and there.

The intimacy of this walk is driving me crazy. I can't wait until we part ways. Or *are* we going to part ways? I'm not going back to the restaurant after this session. I'm going home. I wonder if he's going home too.

We stop, and I keep my eyes on Achilles's hand and not his face as he presses a lit button next to a dark wooden door. I can't hear the bell ring behind the wood, but not even two seconds pass before the door opens, and we're greeted by a petite, elderly woman with curly red hair and the spritely energy of someone probably half her age.

The relationship expert's name is Sophie Brandt, and she has keen eyes that seem to not miss a thing. It's as if she's assessing us as she offers us water, noticing how far away we're standing from each other. It's like her brain is constantly taking notes.

I say I want water, and Achilles doesn't. Once we're seated, Dr. Brandt's assistant hands me a bottle.

"Treasure." She says my name like she's spoken it all her life. "Please tell Achilles what makes you happy."

I stiffen as I gape at the tiny woman's face. I hadn't expected that to be the first question she'd ask. I thought she would spend a little more time breaking the ice, but nope. She's getting right down to it.

"What makes me happy?" I repeat.

She sits back in her chair and interlocks her fingers atop her lap. "Yes."

I can feel his eyes on me, and I want to melt into the burnt-orange leather sofa that we are sitting on.

"I don't know," I say, wanting to fan the flush out of my cheeks. Why in the world am I so discombobulated by this question?

Surely sensing my discomfort, Dr. Brandt says, "I'll help you. Close your eyes."

I'm still looking at her when she nods, ensuring me that she's leading me down the right path.

I close my eyes, and she asks me to inhale deeply. I do that too.

"After you slowly release your breath, speak the answer to what makes you happy."

I inhale, and after releasing my breath, I actually have clarity. "My friends make me happy. And so does my cousin Paisley. I guess good people make me happy." I open my eyes, and she points to Achilles. Oh, I'm supposed to tell him.

The way he's peering at me makes my stomach flutter and heart dance. But I do not show that he's having this effect on me.

"Good people who are nice, kind, and I like them and they like me," I say, staring into his gorgeous eyes. *Unlike you.*

"And you, Achilles?" Dr. Brandt's voice is soft and encouraging.

"Making sure my family is safe," he says without pause.

The way he's looking at me—is he sending me a message too?

"Same," I snap back.

"Your favorite color, Treasure?" Dr. Brandt asks in the same calming voice. "And keep your eyes on each other. You're doing well."

"All of them," I say because that's the truth.

I'm surprised by how the right corner of Achilles's mouth plays with a hint of a smile. I think he liked my answer.

"Achilles?" Dr. Brandt asks.

"Red." The way his eyebrows quirked up ever so slightly. I feel as if there's a salacious meaning behind his answer. And I'm certain it has nothing to do with me. However, I can see it. He has a racy side. *Hmm...*

"And Achilles, what do you like most about Treasure?"

"Her sense of humor," he says without pause.

I gape at him as my jaw drops.

"And Treasure, what do you like about Achilles?"

I'm still speechless and confused. "You think I'm funny?" I thoughtlessly ask.

Achilles answers with a brisk nod.

"Treasure, let's stay on track," Dr. Brandt says. I'm surprised she's so dogmatic about this little exercise we're doing.

I think there's a method to her madness, and it's not as if I don't have an answer to her question, because I do. However, I'm not certain if I want to let Achilles know that even though he's bossy, I like it.

I turn to Dr. Brandt, who actually has her eyes closed. "Can we circle back for an answer?" I say, spinning my index finger.

"No," she says calmly and asks the question again. "The truth, Treasure. The truth."

Achilles hasn't stopped watching me, and his eyes appear to be laughing at me too.

"He's responsible, reliable. I like that," I quickly say.

Then his eyebrows quirk up as our staring transitions into something deeper. I can kiss him. I want to kiss him. My lips fight the urge to do it.

"Achilles, what was your favorite subject of study during high school?" Dr. Brandt asks, not missing a beat.

"Math," he says.

Damn it. His answers are so quick. He's good at this.

"Treasure?" she asks.

"Home economics," I say, attempting to be just as swift with my answers.

His left eye narrows. "Really?"

He seems very surprised. I nod. "I didn't open a restaurant for the money. I like to cook."

He grunts thoughtfully. "So do I."

"The both of you attended university, yes?" Dr. Brandt asks. Her eyes are still closed and enfolded fingers sitting demurely on her lap.

"I dropped out of university," I admit.

"Why?" she asks.

"I hated it."

"Why?"

It suddenly dawns on me that I'm saying all of this to Achilles. Wow. We're actually having our first real conversation, even if it's being guided by a third party. But the only person who knows the answer to that question is my cousin Paisley. And it wasn't as if I had true insight into why I made my decision and shared it with her. Paisley was the one who told me why I left college.

"Because I can't be contained," I whisper to Achilles. "I love the world. I want to experience everything, all the time. At least…"

I drop my eyes from his open gaze. Even though I saw no judgment and no indication that he's weary of me, I couldn't tell him more.

"That's all," I say.

"And you, Achilles?" Dr. Brandt says.

"'At least' what?" Achilles asks.

I look up, overwhelmed by his curiosity. "What?" I ask.

"You were going to say something else. What was it?"

"Nothing," I say. "Forget it."

He's frowning in that way that I loathe again.

"It's fine if Treasure doesn't want to share now. Perhaps she'll do so later," Dr. Brandt says. I'm grateful that she's letting me off the hook. "And Achilles, what was your favorite subject at university?"

He's still frowning. I think he's pouting because he's not getting his way. I wonder when Dr. Brandt is going to ask what we don't like about each other. I would say just that—he's controlling and pouts when he doesn't get his way.

"Business law," he says, and there's an edge in his voice.

"Treasure, where do you see yourself in the next five years?" she asks now that we're back on course.

I don't rush to answer. I don't think I want to share that information with him. Does she know we're getting fake married? And the way he's looking at me seems odd. It's a Max look. Whatever I say, he's ready to use it to his advantage.

I can bullshit him.

"Married with kids," I say, choosing to do just that, bullshit him.

Achilles blurts out a laugh. "You see, she's really funny. What are you hiding, Treasure?"

My eyebrows flash up as my body jumps into fight-or-flight mode. "Sorry?"

"Married with children? You? You're lying."

"Achilles?" Dr. Brandt says in a gentle but chastising tone. "You're taking us off track."

Glaring at him, I ask, "Why are you so sure I'm lying? You don't know me that well." I point to Dr. Brandt. "Does she know the truth?"

He blinks at me like he's furious.

"I understand all that I need to know," Dr. Brandt says as she readjusts in her seat. I think she's finally realized that she's lost control of her little exercise.

"You have an out, Treasure. Were you ever going to mention it?"

I fall back slightly, leaning away from him. "An out?"

"You can pay back the trust and nullify our contract."

"Okay," I say, shaking my head. "You signed the same contract I signed. The details were written in black and white." I say that, but I feel as if I'm being a bit of a hypocrite. I didn't read the details before signing. I could've signed over the right to both of my kidneys without knowing. But even though I've been angry at my dad for years, I trusted him. However, Achilles isn't me. I would think a man as controlling as he is would memorize every line of the contract.

His lips twitch like he wants to respond, but instead he presses them into a very hard line. I fight the urge to make him explain why he believes I'm going to double-cross him. I do plan on paying back the trust to be free of the contract, but I wouldn't just wake up one day and without any warning say, "Achilles, I'm done. *Sayonara.*" I'm not Max or my dad or even Xan. I would warn him first.

Then it occurs to me. I have to picture Max's face whenever I see Achilles because they are just as sharklike when it comes to money and business. He's looking into my affairs—the asshole. I wish I could blow up and tell him to go to hell, but I can't. First of all, it's not my style. Secondly, my restaurant is dropping slowly into a sinkhole, forcing me to play along to get along.

Damn it!

"Let's both take a breath and then reset," Dr. Brandt says.

But I've lost patience. I raise a finger in objection. "I'm sorry, Dr. Brandt, what is the purpose of this exercise?"

She says it's to build a rapport between us so that we'll know how to make easy and pleasant conversation.

I shoot to my feet, ready to storm out and call a cab. "But I don't think he's capable of engaging in an easy and pleasant conversation."

Achilles stands up. His movement reminds me of a bent tree miraculously rising to stand tall. "Listen, I'm sorry. Sit, Treasure. Let's finish this."

I sigh wearily. Why must every encounter with Achilles Lord take so much out of me? And is he really "sorry"? I doubt it. I'm certain his apology is merely a means to an end. But he's a smart guy. It'll be wise for me to follow his lead and get a grip. He's in the big leagues, and if I want to come out of this whole marriage arrangement unscathed, then I need to behave like a formidable opponent and not a brat who throws a tantrum to get her way.

"No, I'm sorry for losing my cool," I say and then sit back down. Cool, calm, and collected as always, Achilles joins me on the sofa. His nearness all of a sudden makes my blood warm. But I know I must say it first just to demonstrate to him that not only am I an adult, but I behave like one too. So I point a hand at Dr. Brandt and say, "Please, Dr. Brandt, let's continue."

OUR SESSION IS OVER. RAIN THAT WAS NOWHERE in sight an hour ago pours down on the car that Achilles and I are sharing. He's not going back to the office. We're going home together, and I'm not sure that's such a good idea. The end of our session couldn't have gone more smoothly. Achilles's favorite meal is simply a broiled steak, rare, with a baked potato. His favorite famous person is Martin Luther King Jr.

"A man has to be in touch with the divine parts of himself to accomplish what he accomplished," he had said.

My panties got even wetter.

I felt pressured to come up with a favorite famous person just as courageous. But instead of Gandhi or Florence Nightingale, I said, "Julia Child because she made me want to be her."

Achilles frowned as if he thought I was a loser for naming a chef. But screw him. Since our whole relationship is built on a lie, I prefer to tell the truth as much as I can.

But yet again, we are alone in the back seat of his chauffeured car, and we've brought with us the sort of sexual tension that looking into each other's eyes while answering personal questions produces.

Achilles is the first to make a phone call and talk business in an attempt to reset our relationship to something less intense and more casual. His replies are short and cryptic. It's apparent that he still doesn't trust me. Instead of twiddling my thumbs as I try to withstand this odd sensation in my chest that feels like butterflies fluttering their wings, I call Paisley, and just as it was before she purposely started avoiding my calls, she answers after the first ring.

"What the hell, Pais," I grumble, keeping my voice as low as possible.

"How are you?" She sounds worried.

I roll my eyes. "Fine."

"I heard you were sick at Sunday night's dinner and Achilles took you home. I've been calling him, checking in on you."

I steal a peek at Achilles, and he's watching me.

"Yeah," I say with a sigh. "I caught a virus. But you knew about Gran's grand announcement and didn't give me a heads-up. Shame on you. I thought you were my better half."

Her chuckle warms my ear. Gosh, I need her right now. "I'm so sorry, Treasure. You know how hard it was to keep the news from you. Grandmother made me promise. She wanted to be the one to tell you and everybody else. Do you forgive me?"

I roll my eyes as if she knows the obvious answer. "Always." I glance at Achilles again. *Why in the hell is he staring at me that way?* I don't think he knows he's doing it. Maybe I should snap my fingers in front of his face to wake him up. Maybe he thinks I'm secretly plotting and planning against him. He's so paranoid. To send him a message, I aim my back at him and whisper, "So when am I going to see you? Are you in town?"

She says they are and that she and Hercules can have dinner with us tonight. I don't even hesitate for a moment when I say, "Absolutely." Then I repeat exactly what she's said in my head. *Wait. Dinner with us?*

Dinner with Friends

TREASURE GROVE

About an hour later, we're seated around the table. Hercules's penthouse is almost an exact replica of Achilles's, only this place has more of a sterile contemporary vibe with its stark white furniture and contrasting black decorative pieces. I'm certain Paisley had no problem adapting to the decor. Her tastes also lean toward what's presented.

The elevator ride up was torturous. Achilles was standing so close while we both kept our focus pinned to the upward counting numbers. I had no idea what was going on inside his brain, but I struggled to keep my breaths fluid while managing to appear calm. But my insides reeled from the pronounced attraction that I've been feeling toward him lately. I keep reminding myself that he's a good-looking man—any woman would give him a second and third glance. However, we can never get naked and do it, and we'll never be friends. As a matter of fact, I'm one hundred percent sure that he'll soon do or say something tonight that will remind me that he is a certified asshole. That always brings me back to my senses.

Dinner started promptly. It has been reported the city is in the crosshairs of a fast-moving superstorm. Barbara Townsend and catering staff must leave in less than two hours. So instead of six courses, we'll have three.

It's not just the four of us either. I was pleasantly surprised to see that Lake and her fiancé, Mason, have joined us. The appropriate greetings were made with hugs, handshakes, and double kisses. I told Mason that it was great to finally meet him. However, his health difficulties that Lake has been supporting him through are obvious in his appearance. His black hair is such a jarring contrast to his sickly pale skin. And he's very thin, not in a healthy kind of way but in a skin-hugging-his-bones kind of way.

I noticed, too, that when Achilles shook Mason's hand and then drew him in for an extra hug, he appeared jarred by Mason's physical condition. I do detect empathy emanating from Achilles. *Damn it.* That's not a quality that makes me dislike him, and I need to dislike him.

The table is set differently than it was at Xan and Heart's house. Men are seated on one side of the table and women on the other. So at one end, Paisley is across from Hercules, who's in the kitchen chatting with Barbara Townsend. Mason sits across from Lake, who's on my right. Achilles is seated across from me. I wonder if I preferred it when he sat beside me, because now I have an unobstructed view of his perfectly handsome face.

Paisley has asked Lake about her upcoming gallery, which will feature a piece they collaborated on. As Lake talks about the computerized portion of the abstract art, it doesn't occur to me that Achilles and I are staring at each other until he sits back in his chair and folds his arms.

Shit. I glance down at my plate as my heart beats like crazy. *What just happened?*

Thankfully, Hercules reenters, stealing all of our attention, and announces that dinner will start now.

Chef Barbara Townsend, barely five feet tall with keen eyes that threaten to show you who's boss if she must, stands at the head of the table, wearing a white chef's coat and hat. A flash of envy blushes through me as she makes her announcement.

First course: New England snow crab cake topped with roasted corn and red pepper ceviche.

THE FOOD IS BEAUTIFULLY PLATED. I INHALE before I dig in. It smells divine, and the first bite sticks the landing. Sounds of enjoyment swim leisurely through the air. Barbara, who is totally satisfied, bows and leaves us to our conversation, which quickly assumes a feverish pitch.

Mason talks about how the union between Hercules and Paisley has changed the mood at Lord Technical Innovations.

Achilles looks like he's chewing on lemons instead of Barbara's unbeatable crab cake. It's clear he doesn't want to have a conversation about their company with me, the Benedict Arnold, at the table.

"That's where the two of you met, right?" I ask to politely change the subject. "LTI?"

"Yes, it was," Mason says enthusiastically.

"Ooh, tell me how it happened," I say with an expression formed by intrigue. I take my second bite of the melt-in-your-mouth first course and simultaneously sense that Achilles has relaxed a bit. He'll probably never trust me.

Lake insists on telling the story of how she spent years trying to win his attention, similarly to all the other girls he dated within the company.

"The rumor was that he was cute but boring, and I thought, perfect, because I'm exciting!"

Her cute sense of humor lands her the perfect amount of laughter. Even Achilles lets one escape.

She says how a week before last Christmas, she invited him to her art exhibit and was surprised he showed up, even though he brought a buffer.

Hercules raises a hand. "That would be me."

Paisley and Lake chuckle.

"He didn't even know I was an artist," Lake says.

"And I sure as hell didn't know she was as popular as she is," Mason says. "But it made a lot of sense. She's a killer interface designer."

"That night, the night of my show, I ditched my own exhibit, and we went on an adventure."

"Through Central Park," Mason adds.

We all watch as they gaze adoringly into each other's eyes.

"It was…" Mason sounds choked up. "All the contours and textures of that night—I'll literally take them to my grave." He appears to force his eyes off the woman he loves and focuses solely on Hercules. "Which will be sooner than we thought."

A smile gradually fades from Hercules's lips as servers enter to collect the plates, but Paisley wisely waves them away and puts her hands together in prayer, signaling to the head server she's thankful for how quickly he sent the others out of the room.

The only men I've ever seen look at each other with such love and appreciation until now are my dad and Xan. Hercules and Mason are definitely bonded. Their eyes are glassy as they just stare at each other, choked up. And nobody says a word because we can feel their emotions deep in our bones. Even I want to cry about the eventual end of their unbreakable friendship.

Mason pulls his shoulders back as he inhales. He's sitting up tall when he reveals, "It's cancer. I have terminal brain cancer." Funny how he said that without his voice cracking. The ease with which the acknowledgment glided off his tongue implies that he truly has come to terms with his condition.

Lake sets her hands in prayer and points the tips of her fingers at Mason. "We cried our hearts out, and now we've decided to live the rest of our days together to the fullest."

Hercules stares at Paisley with this lost look of nonacceptance.

"Anything you want or need, just let us know," Achilles says.

"Well, I'm not quitting my job," Mason says with a soft laugh. But the way his gaze falls to the table is a sign that he's unsure about the claim he just made.

Lake laughs. "Because that job of his is his mistress."

Mason looks at her with tired but flirtatious eyes. "Your lips are my mistress."

Tears stream down Lake's cheeks. I've watched them build in her eyes and was wondering when she would release them.

"Sorry," she says, dabbing her cheeks and eyes with her cloth napkin. "What a bomb you dropped, Lover Boy."

She and Mason chuckle. It's obviously their attempt to lighten the mood.

Eyebrows up, Mason stares at his barely eaten crab cake. "I probably should've waited until the last course to blow tonight's dinner." He turns to Hercules with a smile. But Hercules, who presses the balled knuckles of his fist against his pursed lips, is unable to return the expression.

SECOND COURSE: HERB-CRUSTED LAMB CHOP WITH creamed beets, raspberry, and red wine sauce.

THE RAIN HAS PICKED UP, AND DROPLETS BLAST the window as if they're trying to break the glass. The sound is unsettling but not so much that it disturbs me from cleaning my plate. The good friends at the table have all agreed to banish any more talk of cancer, at least for tonight. Mason, Hercules, and Paisley are now engaging in nerd talk. They're discussing several projects for which Mason is happy he'll be alive to see to the end. I feel Achilles's energy trained on me. I bet he's wondering if I know that they're discussing TRANSPOT.

. . .

THIRD AND FINAL COURSE: PAN-SEARED SCALLOPS topped with mini potato fritters and doused with a white balsamic wine gravy.

WE EAT IT. I'VE NOTICED THAT MASON IS VERY intense about work. Give the wheel to him, and every conversation leads back to LTI. I don't think it's because he's trying to divert our attention from his condition either. I think he's a true workaholic times ten.

The wind has turned stronger, and there have been reports of subway closures. To show our appreciation, Achilles and Hercules dispatch their cars and drivers to take all the servers and Barbara home.

Meanwhile, the men and women break off. We insist that the three men go into the barroom. I think Hercules and Achilles want to have a frank conversation with Mason about his condition and the future.

The ladies head into Paisley's special den. It's not a very girly space. A glass desk and black leather chair are nestled against the tall window.

The desk has papers and books about computer science on top. Paisley has pulled a lot of time in that chair and at that desk. I wonder if she has truly been out of town for all of those weeks. However, she has a matching sofa set on the opposite side of the room and full coffee bar, which is where we lounge.

Paisley makes us what she calls her "special vanilla honey latte" as Lake and I make ourselves as comfortable as we can on the sofa. I find the rain and wind beating on the window while this high in the sky unbearable. But I have so much catching up to do with my cousin and friend that I try to ignore the anxiety that's trapped in my shoulders and back.

"So, how are you holding up?" I ask Lake, caressing her face gently.

"We're fine," she replies in a high-pitched, overly optimistic tone of voice. It's the kind of voice people use when the opposite is the truth. "Yep, we decided to move forward as if everything is okay in the world. Otherwise, we'll be unhappy, and Mason and I are gleefully in love and blissfully happy." Her sigh is layered with sorrow. "This is what Mason wants. And I want what Mason wants because he should be happy, right? Right." She ends that short soliloquy with a forced smile.

I twist my mouth thoughtfully as I regard her body language. For some reason, I'm getting *do not proceed* from her. "Right," I barely say.

When she snaps her attention from me to smile vacantly at Paisley, I know for certain that she doesn't want to hear any comment I might have on how they've chosen to deal with her fiancé's condition.

Paisley avoids looking at me and thereby answering the question in my eyes which asks, *How worried about Lake should we be?* She's treating Lake with kid gloves. And I guess I'll follow her lead because she's better at it than I am.

"How's married life, Pais?" Lake asks, stretching her legs on the cushion of the chaise and crossing her ankles. She has the appearance of repose, and I find it reassuring. Lake usually functions at a higher state of emotional intelligence than rest of us. Maybe she and Mason have unlocked the secret to how to stay blissfully happy during the short time they have left together.

Paisley carefully carries two coffee cups to us. The rich scent of espresso makes love to my senses.

"It still baffles me how I could be so lucky," she says as she carefully hands Lake a cup and then me.

"They're so good together," Lake says.

Paisley trots back to the bar fetch her own cup of coffee. "I know, right? From high school to this, it just blows my mind."

"And Heart isn't pushing you to have a real wedding?" I ask.

Paisley grunts as she rolls her eyes. "You're talking about my mom here."

I raise my eyebrows. "You're right." I laugh softly, remembering that Xan and Heart were married at the courthouse downtown.

Lake sets her cup of coffee onto her lap. She's shaking her right leg.

"Well, I'm sure they approve. He is Hercules Lord," Lake chuckles. "He's number two in a million. Mason is number one."

Paisley laughs as she makes herself comfortable on the left-chaise part of the sofa.

"And he was her first. Did you know that?" Lake looks at me with gaping eyes.

I snort, grinning at Paisley. "Oh, yes, I remember when it happened. There's something cosmic about their relationship. Fate had a funny way of bringing them together. I'm not surprised they're married. I think they're meant to be."

"And you and Achilles?"

At first, I think Lake is making a statement, but her eyebrows are high and she's waiting for me to elaborate, which means she was asking a question.

"Yep," I say tightly.

"I'm surprised you didn't mention the two of you were together after the fight."

"Hmm," I hum.

Lake tilts her head curiously to one side. "Was your relationship with him a secret?"

"Yep." I take a long drink of my hot latte. I sure hope Lake can take the same hint that she gave me not too long ago.

"Why?" she asks.

I sigh and roll my eyes. *She hasn't gotten the hint.*

"I mean… if you don't want to tell me, that's okay."

I jump as wind slams into the windows like it's angry at the glass. I'm ready to go, and not back to Achilles's place. He lives too high off the ground. I couldn't take all the windows pounding and rain beating. I want to go home to my apartment.

"Because… well… I'll show you," Lake says and then takes her phone out of her very cute gray satin crossbody purse. "You might want to check out this post from *TRM*."

My hands fly to my sides and grasp the sofa. "Wait. Did the building just sway?"

Top Rag Mag

TOO SUDDEN TO BE TRUE

> Rumor has it that Achilles Lord and Treasure Grove met and fell in love in a span of one weekend in Majorca, Spain. Raise your hand if you believe that.

We still haven't seen them out in public together. But on the plus side, sources say that Treasure Grove hasn't been living in her own apartment. It has been confirmed that the couple does live together. However, isn't his large penthouse the perfect place to stage a ruse?

Simon Linney was the first to pose that question to us. The mad actor just can't seem to stop coming to us with fresh and juicy deets.

However, at some point, we'll have to dismiss him as the bitter ex-boyfriend he's turning out to be.

And Simon, guy, that's not a good look for a world-famous actor whose throat women would shove their panties down just for one lick of your hotness.

But for now, the heartbroken actor just can't let it go. He swears we shouldn't take our eye off the ball, because Achilles and Treasure's engagement is faker than a three-dollar bill.

All we have to say to that is: Don't worry, Simon, we're watching. We've got our eye on all those balls.

The Superstorm

TREASURE GROVE

The wind is blowing like crazy, and it's raining so hard that it actually sounds like cats and dogs are slamming onto the roof of the car. So many emotions and thoughts snake around each other inside me. The last thing that worries me is being alone in the car with Achilles, which seems so surreal.

"Are you all right?" Achilles finally asks.

I turn to look at him. His eyebrows are pinched with concern.

"I can't stay in your place," I cry. Just saying that releases some of my anxiety. "I can't sleep that close to a superstorm."

He's watching me in his customarily unsettling way, but I don't care. If anything, his expression is pushing me closer to asking him to just drop me off at my apartment.

"I see," he finally says, stroking his chin. "We're actually staying on the tenth floor tonight."

He says that he's had the furniture from the rooftop brought indoors. Also, protective shutters have been installed over all windows, so I don't have to worry about glass breakages. Plus, if and when the power goes out, the building has a backup generator that transitions smoothly from regular electricity.

"You'll be safe and secure with…" His Adam's apple bobs as he swallows. "Tonight. I should've said something to you earlier to put your mind at ease."

He blinks at me, waiting for me to say something. But this rush of emotion that I'm feeling that is so alien to me keeps me from speaking. Achilles is different than any man I've ever been linked to. He practically nursed me back to health for over twenty-four hours. I was in such a terrible state. He even summoned a doctor to check me out. Simon would've never done that. He would've disappeared and left me to fend for myself.

And now this…

My throat is tight, and now I finally understand why I'm unable to respond. I don't trust him being nice to me. But why not? He's shown me that he's nothing but trustworthy, at least on the surface. The contract, the business between our families, the dubious double-dealings—those are the things that make it impossible for us to have faith in each other.

Then my cell phone rings, and it's Lolly. The staff has been sent home. The restaurant is closed. She and her husband are boarding up the windows, but they can't stay any longer.

"It's terrible outside, Treasure. Nearly all the businesses on our street have boarded up their windows. Shit is flying everywhere. A trash can slammed into the east corner window."

My jaw drops as I inhale sharply. "Is there any damage?"

She sighs in relief. "By the grace of God, no. But there's all kind of crap flying down the street. We have to get boarded up, but Rob and I have to get out. We can't be stranded in the city."

Nodding energetically, I say, "Go, go home now. I'll finish the windows."

"I'm so sorry, Treasure."

"No, it's okay."

I turn to Achilles.

"I have to go to the restaurant."

Without asking extra questions, a look of concern washing over him, he tells Danny, his driver, to take me to my restaurant.

ACHILLES AND DANNY INSIST I STAY OUT OF THE way as they work fast to board up all the windows. I want to help because six hands are better than four, but they handle the tools and the wood with such ease that I feel I'll be more of an obstacle than help.

I watch them through the tinted glass. I'm not sure if Achilles can see me staring at him, but God Almighty, what a man. The sleeves of his shirt are rolled up. Soaked in rain, his black pants cling to his strong thighs. He's got a nice package too. I picture myself doing things to him—sexy things.

I squeeze my eyes shut and whip my head from left to right, freeing myself from such salacious thoughts. Our gazes meet when I open my eyes until Danny plasters the final board against the window.

The jarring way in which our staring was interrupted makes my heart thump like thunder. What is happening between us? I consider a sexual relationship with Achilles—nothing but sex. Could it work between us?

"Treasure," Achilles says, standing near the hostess station. I didn't even hear him come in. "You should get in the car while I lock up."

I start to say that I'll lock up, but he's been in charge ever since we arrived. So instead of saying I can handle it, I nod, retrieve my purse off the hostess station, and hand him the keys.

When he takes them, our fingers touch, and that giddy sensation I felt when we first accidentally touched is back with a vengeance. But he has no clue what's going on inside me. I make sure my face displays nothing but a thankful smile as I say, "Thank you for doing all of this. I'm dry. You're wet." I chuckle at my observations. "I really appreciate it."

He's silent and towering over me like a protective wall. Expectation hangs in the air. Releasing a shuddering breath, I don't break eye contact, constraining the urge to kiss him.

Then he takes a step back, and I immediately feel the effect of his distance, and he says, "You're welcome."

THE RIDE BACK TO ACHILLES'S PENTHOUSE TEEMS with sexual tension. At least on my part. Maybe it's just me who's sexually drawn to him and not the other way around which is a good thing. If I assume the lust is a one-way street, I won't lose my head and do something stupid like throw myself at him. But goodness gracious, he ripples with sex appeal. I can still picture his arm and thigh muscles flexing when he reached high up to drill. Having someone like Achilles nearby is shaping up to be quite useful, even if the circumstances that brought us together suck. I must never forget that I need to get out of this contract as soon as possible. Sex will only make me lose focus, and I can't lose focus.

"Thank you," I say, my brain void of a more creative response.

"You've already thanked me," he replies. I've come to learn that the barely visible lift of the corner of his mouth is indeed some sort of smile that just might be flirtatious.

I drop my face to chuckle bashfully. I don't want us to stop talking because sitting in silence feels like a low form of emotional torture. When I look up, our eyes meet. "And you and Danny worked so fast. I would still be there trying to figure out how to work the drill."

His eyebrows flash up in response, but his lips betray no emotion.

"You should have security shutters installed. I know someone," he finally says.

I screw up one side of my face thoughtfully as the dollar signs flash in my head. "I don't know. It's another expense."

He throws up a hand as if to say, *Stop worrying*. "I'll handle it," he says. "Also, your doors should have a security system built into the locks. That way, you'll know who comes in after you've closed."

I sigh as I see more dollar signs. "You're right, of course. And no worries, I'll pay for it all." I'll just use funds from my personal account.

"It's no problem, Treasure. I understand that you're saving because you have bigger plans." The right corner of his mouth plays with that flirtatious smile again. Although, I think he's half teasing and half calling me out.

Drawing air in slowly through my nostrils, I gnaw restlessly on my bottom lip. He's done so much for me lately that I would feel like an awful, entitled user if I didn't explain. "About my opportunity to nullify our contract…"

His eyebrows are up. He's listening, waiting to hear whatever I'm going to say.

"It's not you. Well…" I scrunch my nose and mouth in a finicky manner. "Not anymore. I mean, not since you boarded my restaurant's windows and fed me electrolytes at my lowest moment." I grace him with a full-fledged smile.

I watch my joke land as Achilles smiles.

Good. Now that he's all softened up, I can admit the truth. "It's my dad and uncle. To them, it's almost as if nothing's off-limits when it comes to succeeding in the name of getting ahead in business." I sigh. I can't say what I really feel about them to Achilles. After all, I got the sense that even though we have this contract between our families, there isn't a true cease-fire between the Lords and Groves. "I just don't understand why you've agreed to do this deal."

He narrows an eye thoughtfully. "You don't understand the agreement between us."

"Not really." But I raise my hands, palms toward him. "But I don't want to understand it. I needed the money, Achilles. I was on the verge of losing my restaurant." All those icky feelings of failure come rushing back into me. "And even now, I'm losing a lot more money than I'm profiting. This will all be over before I'm able to pay the trust back. So you can stop worrying about me leaving you and my family in the lurch."

His lips part slightly as if he wants to say something. Then the car stops in front of a metal garage door that rolls up. The drama of driving inside, our wheels getting situated on a lift, and the lift hoisting us up to the building rudely steals my attention. My stomach drops a smidgen, and I press my hand against my belly.

"You don't trust your father?" he finally asks.

I'm taken aback by his question. I should think more before I answer, but my defenses are down. I really don't like the way it feels to be lifted high off the ground in a car. It just feels so wrong, like a human invention that's gone too far.

"Huh?" I ask, staring at the wall beyond the window.

"Treasure, relax, you're fine."

I shake my head. "Why do you need all of this shit? What's wrong with a nice cottage near a lake? I also wonder how healthy it is to live seventy-eight stories above Earth's gravitational pull."

And just like that, he reaches out to gently rub my thigh. His touch is not sexual. It's soothing and comforting. "You'll be fine."

Finally, the car comes to a stop, and I relax a bit.

"You've never lived in a high-rise?" he asks.

"Never," I ardently claim. "I never felt safe residing in any space that's beyond the third floor."

The garage door rolls up, and when light floods the car, it's as if Achilles comes to, and he quickly takes his hand off my thigh.

"I see," he says, stroking his chin thoughtfully. "I see."

***

I went straight to bed. The storm has fully blossomed, and wind gusting and whistling and hurling rain at the glass makes me toss and turn.

Even though my bed is comfortable, I've been trying to fall asleep for God only knows how long.

I reach out to take my cell phone off the nightstand and press the side button to activate the screen. Two hours and thirty-three minutes—that's how long I've been trying to fall asleep. Honestly, I'm not certain the weather is the sole cause of my restlessness. Earlier, Achilles and I went up to his penthouse. He waited for me in the foyer as I put a bag together. Standing in my enormous closet, I could feel the building swaying, which made my stomach queasy. I didn't delay as I threw facial cleanser, fresh underwear—*especially fresh underwear*, because the panties I had on were soaking wet thanks to Achilles—and other essential items along with my favorite pajamas into an overnight bag.

I lie very still in bed as I recall the way Achilles looked at me after I descended the stairs and said, "I'm ready—like, so ready."

I'm starting to comprehend that the way he frowns at me has nothing to do with hostile feelings toward me. I think to him, I'm like a puzzle he has to put together, and he doesn't have the instructions. Basically, he's trying to figure me out.

So I've decided to stop taking his glares personally.

We said goodnight to each other. I bet he's out like a log right now. He's not thinking about me at all or worried about the rain. We're in his universe, after all, not mine, and that is probably why I can't find any peace tonight.

I flip onto my side and smash a pillow over my head. Maybe this will do it.

Closer and Closer

ACHILLES LORD

I can't sleep for shit. I can't stop thinking about how she chews on her bottom lip when she's thinking or the way she stared at me while Dan and I boarded up her windows. Nero's plan is working too well. I'm supposed to make her feel safe with me.

"She's a single girl," Nero said. "Make yourself useful. Just don't use your cock. That's the surest way to blow up this deal."

I made him elaborate on whatever the hell he meant by making myself useful. He said to be nice to her and let her friend zone me. "Guys don't know this, but the friend zone is the securest place to be in a woman's life. Women are loyal as hell to you when you're in their friend zone."

I thought he'd lost his mind. Not because he's wrong—there's a lot of sense to what he said. But I thought Treasure and me becoming friends would be impractical. I'm not certain about that anymore. I couldn't have planned for Treasure to become ill on the night of the big family dinner. Her fever spiked after I got her in bed. She was delirious. She kissed me again and doesn't remember doing it. I wonder if I should take her down memory lane.

I want to use my cock, though.

But Nero was right about that. When shit goes awry, because it will go awry, sex will only complicate matters. But damn, her skin is so soft. Her nearness is overwhelming. I went to bed with another case of blue balls and was forced to do something about it. I've always prided myself on being a man who didn't need to tug one out. I either fuck or don't fuck—and only mild mastur-bation. I think she's figured out I have control issues. I bet that turns her off.

There's a soft rattle on my door, and I sit up.

"Yeah," I call out and reach over to turn on the reading lamp next to the headboard.

It can only be one person, and as the door creeps open, Treasure, who's wearing pink-and-white pin-striped pajamas, takes a few steps into my room, hugging herself.

"Are you awake?" she whispers.

She said she was hungry, so I put on a robe and we went down to the kitchen. She sits timidly on the stool, shaking her leg nervously, and when thunder crashes, she jumps. I'm making two feta omelets with spinach.

There's another crash of thunder, and she leaps off her stool and onto her feet.

"Toast," she says. "I'll make toast."

I want to pull her close to me and whisper, "Are you really afraid of a little thunder, baby?" I want to assure her that I'll die before I let anything happen to her. And then we'll say, fuck the omelets. I'll take her to my bed and do all the shit to her I've been fantasizing about. *But sex will complicate things between us.* I have to remember that.

Finally, the omelets are made and the toast browned. I get the marmalade someone gifted me once—I can't remember who—and we sit at the island and eat.

"Wow," she says after swallowing. "This is really good."

I put my thumb up and thank her. She looks at my thumb like she wants to touch it.

"Can I ask you something?" she says and then feeds herself another mouthful of my omelet.

"Like what?" Her questions can at times be outlandish.

Her chuckle is like music to my ears and enchanting to my cock.

She frowns curiously. "Where's your father?"

My body jerks upright. Shit, another outlandish question. I consider whether I should answer or not. Could she use whatever I tell her against me? Could Max use it against me? My mind quickly travels down all avenues that can lead to harm. She's not close to Max, though. I've been informed that she doesn't like him much at all. But they're family.

"It's okay if you don't want to answer," she says.

At this time of night, her skin is dewier than usual. I allow my gaze to drop to her firm nipples poking her nightshirt. I wonder how they'll feel against my tongue. How will she respond when I suck them?

I shrug indifferently. "My father lives on a tropical island. He owns a restaurant that makes terrible food but great drinks, and he likes it there."

She says, "Hmm," as she nods thoughtfully. What the hell is she thinking? I want to know now.

"How long have he and Marigold been divorced?"

"They're not divorced." Shit. I let that slip.

Her eyebrows quirk up. "No?"

I press my lips. I'm not saying it twice.

"But you've been the man of the house for many years, no?"

I jerk my head back. "Man of the house?"

"Well, yeah. You're obviously in charge of Orion and your mom, and I believe Hercules too. Paisley told me…" Then she catches herself.

So they do talk and share.

It doesn't look as if she's going to back down from whatever she was going to say. It looks as if she's reframing her words. That's why I wait patiently. I want to hear whatever she's going to say.

"Hercules was supposed to marry Rain

Mueller, his cousin, your cousin?" Tilting her head, she waits for a response.

"What of it?" Everybody knows that, which is why I have a sneaky feeling she's dropping crumbs, leading me to the bear trap.

"But you're the oldest. Why him and not you?"

What the fuck.

"Why does it have to be me? Marrying off the eldest son or daughter is an outdated trope, don't you think?" I pull one side of my mouth up into a smirk as I watch her eyes dance with amusement. I'll like bringing that expression on her face to bed with me tonight when I rub one out. Because shit, I'm hard again.

"Yes," she agrees. "It is an old trope. Did you have a girlfriend?"

And there it is—the big reveal. Did Hercules know about me and Penelope, and if he did, why in the hell is he sharing it with Paisley?

"Is that what Hercules told Paisley?" I ask.

Her head tilts as she watches me while smiling. Then she sits up straight and cuts a bite-sized portion of her omelet with her fork. "Well, if it's any consolation, I can't picture you in love with anyone. And no, that's not what Paisley told me. I was just fishing."

I don't believe her, but while silence prevails, I let the subject at hand drop. I'll get in touch with Herc later to ask him what the fuck she's talking about.

But I'm still troubled by something else she said.

"You can't picture me in love?"

She casually shakes her head as she finishes swallowing. "Why do you look at me the way you do?"

I like her style of rarely ever answering a direct question. I would guide her back on the path to answering what I asked, but I'm intrigued by this new path we're traveling.

"How do I look at you?"

She points to my face. "Like that?"

Maybe it's because I want to fuck you silly but can't. "I can't see what you're talking about."

"It's like you hate me."

That's ridiculous. "I don't hate you. I don't know you well enough to hate you." Now it's my turn. "But what about you… are you still carrying on with Simon Linney behind my back?" Warmth rushes to my eyes, and I'm grinning, enjoying whatever kind of game we're playing.

She blushes as she curls her body, pushing her hip up. It's a seductive pose, but she's more cute than sexual. "I'm a faithful and loyal lover, Mr. Lord." She uncorks her body to point at my face. "And wow, Mr. Lord, that's a very real smile you're gracing me with."

Shit, I am grinning, and I shake my head because of it.

"No," she says. "I carry no torch for a serial cheater like Simon. I actually caught him and Cherry Attwell fucking—like, butt naked and going at it like wild animals in nature." Frowning contemplatively, she presses a finger against her chin. "And when I saw them, I didn't think, 'Oh my God, my fiancé's screwing around, and it hurts.' No… I thought, 'Shit, I can't walk away from this catastrophic situation, because I need the money.'"

Her whole demeanor has changed. She's less playful and flirtatious. But I'm fond of the more serious and thoughtful side of her too.

"I crept out of his trailer, thinking, 'How can I use what I just learned about him to get the hell away from him and still be paid what's owed to me?' And poof, there was my dad. You know what I call that?"

I shake my head. It's amazing how she has my complete attention.

Smirking, she says, "Divine intervention. I think it's all going to work out, Achilles. You're going to get what you want, and I'm going to get what I want. And you will live happily ever after, and so will I."

I rub my chin. That's cute. My heart skips a beat because she's so fucking cute. "Perhaps."

"What do you want, Achilles? What will give you that sense of living happily ever after?"

I tense up and then resume eating. She's getting too personal, especially since I've never given what she asked any thought.

But since we're being honest, I say, "There is no such thing."

I steady myself for her rebuttal, but one doesn't come. I glance at her, and she's facing her plate, eating too.

"I agree," she finally says. "I said that wrong. I meant happy in the moment."

Humph, I grunt. I've already said too much.

We eat in silence, and since it's quiet, the rain is louder and so is the wind. There's fear in Treasure's eyes when she glances over her shoulder and in the direction of the windows.

"Achilles?" Her voice is hoarse and low.

"Yeah," I whisper.

"Can I sleep with you tonight?"

I jerk myself back so hard that I almost fall off my stool.

"Just tonight, I promise. I'll stay on my side of the bed. I promise."

Treasure Grove

If it were any man other than Achilles Lord, I wouldn't be so surprised he let me into his bed. But I had to ask. I wouldn't have been able to get through the night alone in that dark room with the wind growling and rain clawing angrily at the windows. The shutters make nature's fury easier to endure, but not that much easier. But look at him. My eyes have adjusted to the dark. I want so badly for him to bring me near. To feel his cock pinched against my ass. That alone would probably make me orgasm several times.

But look at him…

Achilles snores, but it's not hard, rigid snoring. It's a soft, hypnotic sound. The elements are still taking their rage out over the city, but that's not why I can hear my heartbeats pounding in my ears. Is this what contained lust feels like? I've never had to deny my lust. Every man I ever wanted, wanted me three times more. A few have even come before thrusting inside me. But Achilles is as snug as a bug in a rug, sleeping on the opposite side of his king-sized bed with two fluffy pillows stacked under his head and his warm comforter and sheets pulled up to his neck. He reminds me of how husbands and wives slept in those very old movies.

I close my eyes finally. Achilles is never going to fuck me. Maybe the rumors are true—maybe he is gay.

MUTED DAYLIGHT FILLS THE ROOM. WELL, IT'S not too muted. I can't hear a trace of rain or wind, and a very, very hard body is against my backside.

Instead of one, I open both eyes. I don't want to move an inch, which means I can't look down to see that Achilles's arms are actually around me and securing me against him.

Yes!

I vaguely recall tossing and turning as more wind slammed against the window. Then, I rolled several times until we were touching, and now I'm in his arms. And yes, pressed against my ass is a humongous boner.

Then it all happens so fast.

Achilles moans as he lodges his erection deep into the crack of my ass. His prod is so vigorous.

"Mm…" he moans as his hand moves under my blousy nightshirt, and I sigh when his palm makes contact with my skin. Up his hand travels, and I am quivering, squeezing my thighs to relieve the tickling sensation in my lady parts.

Achilles cups my breast, compressing my roundness, indulgently and gradually working his way to the nipples, and squeezes.

"Ooh…" I sigh.

His hand freezes. I feel his body tighten against me.

"Shit," he mutters. And just as soon as he says, "I'm sorry," his body abandons mine.

I don't move a muscle as I listen to his feet

pounce against the hardwood floor. Then he's in the bathroom. He closes the door.

I touch myself. I'm so very wet. He wanted me. I want him. I can stay in bed and let him have me. But he stopped himself when he could've just taken me. Achilles is not a timid man who waits for opportunities to come to him. He takes what he wants. This I know. I can sense. He is that man. But he didn't take me.

Hercules had told Paisley that he thought his brother was in love with a woman. He went right to my lady parts—her lady parts.

I slide out of his bed, regretting ever asking him to let me sleep in his bed. Because now I know Achilles Lord has been intimate with a woman. So much so that he has sexual moves he uses on her to get her hot and wet and ready for morning sex with him. Oh, what a lucky girl.

Friend-Zoning?

TREASURE GROVE

I collapse on my bed, my body reeling from what just happened. How did that happen? How did I end up in his arms without realizing it? Usually, when I'm that close to a man, his body heat makes me sweat. He must've taken hold of me not long before I woke up.

I make myself very still as I listen out for any sound. I hear nothing. This place is so big and well-built, it's hard to hear if anybody is in the condo unless they're in the room with me. Regardless of how I feel about what just happened between me and Achilles, I'm so relieved that the rain and wind have vanished. I'm not hungry after eating Barbara's dinner last night and then Achilles's omelet, which for some

253

reason, even though it wasn't half as tasty as Barbara's dishes, I'd eat a million times over.

"I like him." I confess to the tepid air sitting around me.

I yawn and then absentmindedly crawl under the luxurious sheets and duvet. I cuddle up with the bedsheets, reliving how it felt to have Achilles's hands on me. Before long, and after one last yawn, I fall asleep.

I WAKE UP A LOT LATER. I HAVE NO IDEA WHERE Achilles is in the house. I'm too nervous to go looking for him. I mean, he felt me up this morning, and I wanted him to go all the way. I shouldn't want that. I can't have that. But it's late in the afternoon, and I'm hungry. I don't want to risk running into him in the kitchen, so I call room service. I order a seafood Cobb salad and work from bed today. It's still raining out, but the weather isn't as bad as it was last night.

Nya and I narrow down the menu. It's too large and expensive. It takes us hours to complete the task. Nya has favorite dishes she refuses to stop cooking because they are her signatures. I couldn't talk her out of doing her cracked noodle beef Bolognese. It's not very popular. The cracked noodle has great flavor but not so pleasant a texture. But it's one of Nya's favorites, so it stays. We'll soon see if the items we've cut will cut some expenses. I hope so.

Next, I call Lolly, who complains about not being included in the call with Nya.

"She knows how to work you, Treasure. She gets you all excited about her fucking expensive menu."

I feel rattled by what Lolly points out because she's right on the money. She says it's the same old script. Nya takes from one dish and adds to another. She's a spoiled chef who doesn't know how to edit. And maybe a flavor explosion in the mouth isn't always preferable. The more I listen to Lolly, the more I'm willing to concede that I'm terrible when it comes to running a business.

We decide to table menu planning until tomorrow. We have more pressing issues with two popular celebrity parties that are on the horizon. Two A-listers are throwing their soirées this weekend, one on Friday and the other on Saturday. My presence has been requested. There's nothing like having a real-life billionaire heiress slinking through the room, greeting invitees, taking selfies with them, making them feel important, because apparently, I'm supposed to be important.

We return to our prior conversation about the cost of their events versus what they're paying.

"Did you go back and ask for more money?" I ask.

"Not yet. We're still working on shaving costs. Give me a few days."

This is ridiculous. As soon as Lolly and I hang up, I saunter to the kitchen to figure out the cappuccino maker. I need caffeine. It'll help me get up the nerve to call Princess Vanessa and Charla Hinkley. I'm going to demand that they pay what they owe. Screw them. I know how to play hard-bitch. I've learned from the best—Max, Xander, and Leo. I gasp inaudibly when I see Achilles at the island, reading papers that look like work documents.

"I put steaks in the oven for us," he says. "If you're hungry. Also"—he checks his watch—"we might want to move back up to the main penthouse in the next two hours. House cleaning will be in tonight."

First of all, he looks so handsome. He's wearing black dress pants, no jacket and a vest, no tie. The man is so hot, he could sink a glacier. My face drops, and so does my heart. "But I like this apartment better."

He's watching me with his customary Achilles grimace until he refolds his sleeves and says, "Well, this unit is primarily used as a guest apartment for business clientele." He strokes his chin. "But I hear you, Miss Grove. Let me work on something."

I'm smiling from ear to ear, and I can't stop myself. It's as if he's chosen to not make it weird between us, but still, it has to be mentioned.

"Okay. And about this morning—it was no big deal."

He inhales deeply then exhales. "But it was a big deal. I shouldn't have touched you without your permission."

"Well… you probably thought I was someone else." My eyebrows quirk up, waiting for him to confirm my suspicion.

After a moment of pause, he whispers, "Right."

And with that one-word answer, my heart free falls. However, I take great pains not to show my distress. But still…

"Well…" I sigh. "If it's any consolation, you have good hands."

I'm rendered lightheaded by his steady gaze. The longer he peers at me as if he's seeing and not seeing all parts of me at once, the more I feel as if I'm crashing into him. Maybe I shouldn't have made that last comment, especially now that I know for sure he believed he was waking up with another woman.

"Thank you," he says softly and without taking his eyes off me.

Dropping my face, I break eye contact to blush. "You're welcome." I take a deep inhale before looking up again. We are trapped by each other's gaze. I should go—I really should.

"How's your day been?" he asks.

Good. He's trying to prolong our interaction too.

"Fine," I reply in a high-pitched voice. Then my optimistic exterior crumbles as all the stress I experienced recently comes roaring back. That's right. I need a coffee. "I just thought I would be making more money, but I'm not. Our spending is through the roof."

Achilles's thoughtful grunt is reassuring. I hadn't

meant to confess that to him. If I had told my dad what I just said to him, he would've grunted too, but it would've been one of pure judgment. And I would've felt it deep in my bones. I would've known that I, Treasure Grove, had fucked up because at some point along the path of growing up, I didn't give Leo Grove's stellar advice enough credence. I'm sure my dad doesn't make me feel that way on purpose, but regardless, he does.

"Never think you have to stick with any business decision that doesn't suit your bottom line," he says.

I feel as if I'm blinking in slow motion as I think about all the mistakes I've made since being paid by the trust until now. I know what they are, and they've grown from the size of a baby dinosaur to that of Godzilla.

"I'll remember that," I mutter.

Achilles nods slowly as familiar energy swirls around us and links us.

To put an end to this shared moment between us, I say very loudly, "By the way, I need coffee, a really good one," and roll my strained gaze around the kitchen in search of the coffee maker Achilles used the other day.

Achilles taps the stool beside him. "Sit, and I'll make you one."

***

THE NEXT MORNING

Last night, Achilles and I talked more about business as we sipped the cappuccinos he made. I'm not surprised that he's a wealth of information. He's stellar at giving advice without making me feel like a fool. He said, "In business, you can't be afraid to make mistakes, own them, and then correct them." Then, I gushed about every single mistake I ever made, like purchasing Treasure Island, for one.

"I wanted to make myself a successful Grove in my own right," I had said and then revealed something that I don't think a proper Grove should ever admit to a Lord. "I love my dad, but I don't trust him, and you shouldn't either. He's like…" I bent my neck to one side to ponder how to put it. "He's like that game hot potato, the one we played as kids."

Of course, Achilles had no idea what I was talking about. So I asked him to put his hands on top of mine. That was my first mistake. The first inkling of skin-on-skin contact, and my body recalled all parts of his hardness against me. After I recovered control of my breaths, I made my hands feel as if they were vibrating under his and said, "This is how safe I feel about this whole deal of ours." And then I slapped the top of his hand before he figured out he should move them off of my shaky foundation.

Faces close, Achilles and I stared at each other for a long time. I didn't have to wonder what he was thinking. The foreboding look in his eyes said it all. Regardless, though, I wanted to strip out of my pajamas and melt my flesh with his just to assure him that I would never do anything to intentionally hurt him. But I also wanted to run and hide away from everything I had just revealed to him. I felt like a traitor.

"How about I come in take a look around the restaurant," he finally said. "Maybe I can help you figure out why you're hemorrhaging cash."

"Okay," I said lowly, past my tight throat and without hesitation.

Then the night cleaning crew showed up, and we journeyed our way back to his penthouse apartment. Despite feeling as if we should kiss goodnight, while in the foyer, I said good night.

He said, "I'll stop by the restaurant in the morning." And then we went to our separate rooms.

I thought I would toss and turn from the urge of wanting him so badly I could burst. But I didn't. After bathing, moisturizing, and then crawling into bed, I fell immediately to sleep.

Achilles must've already left for the day when I woke up and dressed myself smartly in a matching golden yellow skirt-and-sleeveless-shirt set. I chose the breathable cotton outfit because I could see the humidity kissing the windows, and knew that New York City was going to feel like a swamp today.

There's never a need to eat breakfast before coming to the restaurant. The morning staff always makes sure there are scrambled eggs, bacon, danishes, fruit, and coffee for everyone.

I'm now eating at my desk when Hayley, one of the administrative assistants, comes rushing into my office without knocking, skin patchy, eyes deliriously wide with excitement, and says, "He's here. Your fiancé."

I tap down my own excitement as I rise calmly out of my chair to stand. "Thanks, Hayley. Please have him…"

She raises a finger pointedly. "He's brought an

entire work crew, and he wants you to come out and select shutters."

I feel my eyes grow wide as I process what she just told me. "He's done what?"

That's right. He said he would furnish my restaurant with security shutters, but I never thought he would get it done this soon.

———

No wonder Hayley looked so feverish when she broke into my office. Achilles is a vision of yumminess. In the suits he wears, his body expands, curves, and elongates in all the right places.

He watches me approach, making me feel as if I'm on a movie screen in a dark theater and there's no one to look at but me.

"You look pretty today," he says when I'm close.

I look down at my feet to blush before I'm able to thank him. Before I saw him, I was a little unnerved by his boldness. But seamlessly, after one sweet compliment, I'm like putty in his hands. Once I recover from bashfulness, I ask, "Who are all these people in my restaurant?"

Surprisingly, Achilles chuckles. I think I've broken through his defenses. Of course, he reminds me that he said he would install the security blinds and door system.

"I remember," I say. *But I never thought you'd follow through with it*, I don't say.

But he has followed through, and I select a brand that I can lower at the end of the day and will have the aesthetic appearance of opened shutters on the outside windows. When potentially property-damaging weather systems roll in, the blinds will close and lock automatically. Also, if the blinds sense someone is trying to damage them on purpose, an app will send a video to my cell phone and then ask if it or I should call the police. And all the work, every piece of it, will be finished today.

I refrain from throwing my arms around him and mauling him with a deep kiss better than the one I gave him last weekend.

Then Achilles asks me to take him on a tour of the restaurant. It's easier to be near him when I have my business brain on. He asks me a lot of questions that I don't know the answers to. I don't have a tracking system in place for all the supplies that are bought and used in the kitchen and around the restaurant in general. Apparently, I should know how much toilet paper is consumed. He also points out what I already know—the build-out was not a good business decision. I was not in the position to expand yet. And also, a restaurant is a different kind of business than an event hall. He says I should consider incorporating the dance hall into the main restaurant. But first, I have to make sure my menu can accommodate more seating.

We're standing in my office. It's the end of a long and arduous assessment by Achilles. Even though it feels like a two-ton gorilla sits on my shoulder, I know what to do to shrug the beast off me.

"That was a lot," I say, folding my arms across my chest. "I really screwed up, didn't I?"

Achilles's hand flies up like he wants to touch me, but then he thinks better of it. "No, you haven't, Treasure. Now you know what to do. So do it."

I interlace my fingers so that I won't succumb to the urge to grip the back of his neck and pull his lips down to mine. "I will," I whisper, looking at my hands.

"Oh," he says, and I quickly look up. "I'm

going out of town until next week. How about we go out on our date when I get back?"

I count the days in my head. It's Thursday. That means he'll be gone for three days at least. I miss him already.

"Sure, okay," I say as if it's no big deal. I also refrain from asking him if he's leaving town for business or pleasure. However, the question is expanding inside me like a balloon, wanting to burst past my lips.

"But you have a nice establishment here," he adds.

"Thanks. After you, things will certainly change." I chuckle.

"After me, huh?" He's smirking. No... it's more than a smirk. Achilles Lord is, without a doubt, flirting with me.

"So..." I grin coyly. "Are you spending the weekend with the woman you thought you were groping yesterday morning?" Ooh, that was crafty of me and a big score. My breaths slow to a crawl as I wait for his response.

Hallelujah, I made him simper again. "No. I'm not."

"Who did you think you were groping, anyway?" I venture to ask.

"Did you come up with that on your own?" he asks.

I knit my eyebrows thoughtfully. "Come up with what?"

"I never said I thought I was groping another woman. I knew exactly who I was touching, Treasure."

I'm confused. I'm too flustered to play back the conversation we had in the tenth-floor kitchen, but I thought he confirmed that he believed he was groping another woman.

He moves even closer, and our fronts are almost touching. "But hey…" Suspense-filled silence hangs in the air.

I'm completely under Achilles's spell. Bold Treasure Grove, the seductress who caught a slippery trout like Simon Linney and so many playboys like him, would finish closing the distance between me and Achilles. I would tilt my head back, position my lips near his, and breathily whisper, "Yeah?"

But I don't do that. Achilles is a different kind of animal than Simon or even his fickle brother Orion. He's the real deal. The kind of man that can change a girl's life for the better. I've come across guys like him before but never one wrapped in his frosty demeanor and repelling grimaces. Usually, guys who bring an entire crew to your restaurant to install blinds, make cappuccinos to give you advice about your struggling business, and take care of you when you're grossly sick are generally affable and eager to please. Because in the end, they want something in return. They would want me to spread 'em and let him bang too fast and come too early. But Achilles—being so generous to me or anyone else is what he's been conditioned to do. I imagine he had to become a man when he was supposed to be a boy. It makes me want to comfort him, kiss him, and promise that I will never exploit that part of him for my own benefit.

"Remember when you kissed me?" he asks.

I swallow all the brand-new exciting feelings I have for him and say, "Mm-hmm," and then sigh. All the sensitive parts of me feel as if they are floating to him and already interacting with his lust. Because lust is the energy he's radiating.

"How about we do that again?" he says.

Skin sizzling with warmth, I'm experiencing an out-of-body experience as I nod.

There's no hesitation. Achilles presses his solid chest hard against my breasts. Our eye contact remains strong, and I can see his yearning. I know he can see mine. We're on the same page when it comes to living out this moment. Strong and decisive hands grip my waist. Just when I thought we couldn't get any closer, Achilles's unyielding erection compresses the top of my pubis. The pressure united with my arousal launches a faint streak of pleasure through my lady parts.

And his breath is minty, which is evidence that he's been planning this kiss.

"Hi," he whispers.

Forearms strewn across his rocklike shoulders, fingers stroking the back of his neck, my lips part, opening to let him in.

Last time, I kissed him first. This time, even though I can hardly stand the wait, I wait until his lips and tongue make contact with mine.

Oh boy… my head is spinning.

Achilles is a sensual kisser. His tongue is needy but soft and indulgent. His lips are smooth like satin. Moans in ranges of sound I've never heard until now escape me. I'm in such need of him. And our kissing has tilted the both of us way past full, yet we're not clamoring at each other like wild lustful animals. Yet I'm gripped by such an insatiable desire. I am pulling him, squeezing him to me. Tears burn the backs of my eyes. His mouth is beyond delicious. I'm needy for Achilles Lord. My heart just wants to explode with… *oh my God.* With…

No, not that.

Yes—that.

That something feels a lot like love.

Knock, knock, knock.

Our kissing draws to an end, but he still holds me close. He can't let me go yet. My legs are the constitution of jelly. Therefore, if he lets go of me, I just may sink to the floor.

"Ask who it is?" he whispers.

I swallow, nod, and yell, "Who is it?" Despite trying to sound normal, my voice sounded strained, like I'm hiding something.

There's a pause. "It's me, Hayley. The shutters are up. Gino would like to consult with Mr. Lord about the security doors."

I twist my body to stare at the doorknob. It wouldn't be so bad if Hayley found us like this. That would be a good play on our part. But are we still playing? I'm not sure.

Then Achilles lifts his eyes to glare over my head. I study how high his chest rises and how deep it lowers. I've stirred him. He wants me just as much as I want him.

"We'll be right out," he says in a clear, unruffled voice.

Hayley doesn't answer right away, but I sense that she suspects we're doing something sexual in my office. I wonder how far she thinks we've gone.

"I'll see you Monday?" he whispers. Then before I can answer, he kisses me one more time. His lips are still soft, and his tongue tenderly strokes mine.

"Um, okay." Hayley's voice comes through faintly as my head continues to spin from experiencing the best kiss of my entire life.

Top Rag Mag

" *We told you we'd keep you updated with any new news about Achilles Lord and Treasure Grove's union. Well, sources say that the eldest —and, according to a* TRM *staff table poll, the hottest—Lord brother spent all day at his fiancée's restaurant. He even came out in the middle of a superstorm to personally board up the windows of her restaurant. Sources say that the two are definitely in love.*

And we have photos!
See below.

The Engine Roars

TREASURE GROVE

I've been lying in bed, watching *TRM*'s video of Achilles and Danny drilling nails into wood boards. I'm reading the comments section, which continues to expand every second.

A billionaire who will do backbreaking work for his woman has to be breaking backs in bed. Umm… he's sexy.

From loser to winner. Buh-bye, Simon LAME!

You go girl!

A friend who has a friend, who has a friend, told me that they had sex in her office.

My jaw drops as I yank myself out of a bad posture. Holy shit, do we have a mole in our midst? I release a longing, lengthy sigh. Hayley knocked on my office door earlier today. Her pauses were seasoned with assumption. Is she the source of the leak? I think about Hayley, thin, barely five feet tall, with her dark hair unfashionably gathered into a ponytail at the back of her neck. She rarely smiles and is always ready to accept and carry out marching orders. There's no way in the world the leak came from her. But to think that something that happened in my place of business should get back to *TRM?* That comment by someone named BetBeeDoll is quite troubling. I'll have to look into it.

I relax against the headboard. I feel… I don't know, lonely maybe. It's only the first night, and I already miss Achilles's presence.

Not good, Treasure.

He hasn't even called to wish me a good night, which is a further sign that he's not interested in carrying on a bona fide relationship with me. And why should he be? He's a smart man. No matter what's going on between us, I'm still connected to him by way of a contract. He has to keep his wits about him, and so do I.

I darken the screen of my phone and then close my eyes to search inwardly until I find the memory of that haunting kiss in my office. I see us. I feel it. His mouth on mine. His sensual way of tonguing.

"Damn it." I open my eyes.

That little exercise didn't work.

Realizing it's best to just go to sleep and sort out my feelings for Achilles tomorrow, I stretch my arm to sit my cell phone on top of the nightstand, and that's when it chimes. I quickly pull the device back to me to read the screen. With a gasp, I slap a hand over my chest. It's a text message from Achilles.

Good night, TG

I laugh, knowing he's referring to me as TG because Hercules sometimes calls Paisley PG. My fingers get to work fast, typing.

Good night, Mr. Lord

Not even five seconds pass before my phone chimes that it's pregnant with a beautiful new message from Achilles.

Sleep well. I'll call you tomorrow.

Shit. My eyes grow wide as I wonder how cool I should play it. I type.

Great. I'll be counting the minutes.

I sit still, staring at my reply for a few beats. No... I shouldn't say that. I sound too eager—too thirsty. Although, I am thirsty for him. When I returned home for work, I dug my old friend out of my drawer, fell on my bed, drew from memories of our time together, and made myself come over and over and over again.

I delete my last reply and type instead:

Okay. Sleep tight, Mr. Lord.

Seconds tick by, and then those seconds turn into minutes. He's done texting for the night. Twisting my mouth thoughtfully, I wonder if I played it too cool. Maybe I should've sent the more enthusiastic reply.

Disappointed, I get ready to put my phone back on the nightstand until it rings. I swallow a gasp. It's Achilles, and I answer it before my device can ring twice.

"Hello?" I say, my heart thumping like crazy. "I mean"—I touch the warmth flushing across the side of my face—"hi."

"You sleep tight too," he says in a sultry bedroom voice that makes me want him even more.

I swallow and taste my desire. "Okay, I will." I sound strained.

"And you're a magnificent kisser, TG. May I have more of you when I see you on Monday? Well… all of you. I want all of you."

I'm nearly choking on my deepened breaths. It takes longer than it should for me to breathlessly say, "Yes. Yes, you may have all of me."

IT'S FRIDAY, AND I'VE DRESSED, MADE COFFEE AND a fried egg with a quick salsa, and then Danny drove me to the restaurant. I've been preoccupied —so many thoughts of Achilles. Thankfully, my thoughts are my own, and no one else can see or hear them. Without shame, I let myself indulge in everything I relish about Achilles Lord. He has six-pack abs that are visible through his shirts. I will enjoy sliding my fingers up and down the ridges of his abs sooner rather than later. His rich cologne has become a serious aphrodisiac. One sniff, and my cells sizzle. And his eyes on me... oh God, his eyes on me. For so long, I have been confused by what I felt when he looked at me in that special way of his. But now I'll admit that Achilles Lord has never repelled me. On the contrary, the way he stared merely enticed me.

My morning meeting with Lolly moves along swimmingly. While most of our staff bustle about, preparing for tonight's big party, I take Lolly on the same tour of my restaurant that my capable future husband took me on. She's into all the proposed fixes and is excited about the possibility of saving a lot of money. For instance, we already have an inventory system in place. But Lolly admits that the count is off because we don't have an easy way for staff to log used or damaged goods. Then I tell her about smart shelves, a storage system that Achilles suggested. He said that LTI uses them in all of their warehouses. When an item is taken out of a slot on the shelf, the shelf will send the new count to a software system. We make the decision to order and install smart shelves on the spot.

Then Lolly and I go back to her office to crunch the numbers on what we pay versus what we'll spend on my fancy new expansions, the party hall, and the lounge. Four hours later, three things are clear to us. Achilles was right yet again. We need to either absorb the new spaces into the main restaurant or sell or rent the spaces to another business. Achilles actually suggested renting to a business that complements my restaurant. He gave me a number of good ideas and said he'll be able to help me with finding and managing a renter. No wonder I was so hot for him when we made it to my office.

"Wow," Lolly says, tapping her finger on a small corner of her desk that's free of papers. "I think you've said the name Achilles a hundred times."

I drop my eyes to laugh bashfully. "No, I didn't."

"And you're blushing, Treas." She sounds so surprised. "You never blush over a boy."

I can't object even though I want to object. "Well… he's been a lot of help rather than hurt."

"Yeah," she says, sounding sympathetic. "Not like Simon Linney, who turned out to be a real cad."

I snort a chuckle. "Cad?"

She laughs. "I thought I'd make him sound more British."

I'm wavering between smiling and frowning thoughtfully as I recall his fake accent. Even Lolly doesn't know that he's a fake. I almost feel like it's my job to inform her of the truth. But then, that will make me a hypocrite because my association with Achilles is just as fake.

As usual, there are not enough hours in the day. I jump from one task to the next, putting out fires, finally looking Princess Vanessa Downing in her spoiled eyes and saying no, we will not set up confetti to drop from the ceiling at 10:03 p.m., especially since her party starts in less than an hour. No, we will not add an extra strip of blue lights along the red carpet because it'll look cool with the orange and red lights that we've already added that she did not pay for. And no, no, no, I will not make Nya scramble to add caviar with a freshly made truffle chip to the appetizer menu. Of course, she didn't want to pay extra for that request either.

But I played my part by sauntering through the event, greeting her guests while wearing a stunning powder-blue off-the-shoulder silk cocktail dress. So many of the princess's guests wanted to take photos with me. I was reminded of what Ingrid once said, something that I disregarded and attributed to her kissing my ass. People do that, kiss the boss's ass. She said that the celebrities want their parties at Treasures because of me. I'm the draw because I'm a Grove.

I guess I've always known that to a certain degree, but tonight, reflected in Vanessa's attention-starved friends' eyes, I saw it. And I'm not sure I liked it, especially since all I wanted was to be in the kitchen with Nya, who actually made that truffle chip for Vanessa. She thought that using tuna tartar instead of caviar would incur no extra cost. But again, Vanessa hadn't paid for the tuna, so yet again, I lost money on that damn birthday party.

It's late when I arrive at the penthouse, and Achilles hasn't called like he promised. Yes, I'm disappointed and actually surprised that he hasn't. I take Achilles to be a man of his word.

I would call him instead, but my feet hurt and I'm sticky, tired of smiling and pretending to be a Disney Princess heiress for a bunch of people I've never met. Heck, I even learned that I'm a better actress than I thought! If I had made a conscious effort to learn my lines better and get into the role of Raylene Preen, I might have done a better job bringing her to life. Because tonight, my acting was flawless.

I sit in a warm bath and fight the urge to fall asleep. When I've sat long enough in the silken water, I moisturize and enter my comfortable bed. Then when I'm settled between the sheets, like a spark flickering in my head, I consider calling Achilles.

But what would I say to him?

You were supposed to call me, but you didn't. Is that your way of reminding me that I am not a real option for you?

"Maybe it's for the best," I whisper and then squeeze my eyes shut as I shake my head against the pillow.

Eyelids heavy while tears burn the backs of my eyes, I stare at the dimmed light fixture above my bed. I'm so confused by what's happening between me and Achilles. I don't want to be a fool again. Because after the smoke cleared, that's exactly what finding Simon and Cherry screwing made me feel like—a fool.

Closing my eyes, I release the tears I've been holding. This is the first time I've cried over the loss of that shabby relationship. I was going to marry Simon Linney. What in the hell was I thinking? And now I have this thing with Achilles, and he's already saying one thing and doing another. He's already pulling me near and then pushing me away.

A message chimes on my phone. All of a

sudden, I forget how sad I am as I sit up and swipe my device off the nightstand.

I frown at the screen. "The desk of Achilles Lord," I whisper and then open the text.

Mr. Lord apologizes for not calling today. He has traveled out of cell coverage range. However, he will reach out to you as soon as he's able. Mr. Lord says good night and that he can hardly wait to see you.

—Message delivered by Jenn Masterson,

2nd Executive Assistant to Mr. Achilles Lord, Esq.

I hug my cell phone to my chest, over my heart. I'm so relieved to have heard from him—but am I? I hold my phone on my lap and stare at the black covering against the tall windows and think, what will happen when the fast-moving train carrying all the crap that will go wrong one day gets closer? Its engine roars toward us from a distance. I can hear it faintly. Soon, it will collide with me and Achilles, and then what will become of these darling emotions sweeping through me? What will become of us?

The End of the Long Weekend

TREASURE GROVE

SATURDAY

I'm back at the restaurant, and I am working my tail off to institute the new changes that will cost a lot up front but save me a lot more in the long run. Ingrid has reminded me that I'm to make an appearance at tonight's party, but I call her into my office and deliver the news. I will not make an appearance tonight, and Charla Hinkley's party will be the last. We will cancel all other reservations, tell them we apologize, that we are unable to support their events due to structural issues.

"Really, it's the end of all parties? Because last

night's was such a success." Ingrid asks. Her bright eyes are full of disappointment.

"Yes," I say. "And we will begin the rebuild, incorporating the party hall space into the main dining facility next week."

And that starts a whole new conversation about her job duties changing. It's like this for the rest of the day—I meet with staff, and we talk about the changes. I meet with vendors and contractors. By the end of the night, when Charla's party has hit a high note, Danny is driving me home, and my head rests against the back seat as I try so very hard not to miss Achilles.

SUNDAY MORNING

I had a really good night of sleep. I'm not going into the restaurant today. Achilles will be back tomorrow. I can't wait.

I call Paisley to ask if she wants to grab brunch at Treasures. My call goes straight to voicemail. I have a sneaking suspicion she is wherever Achilles is. It now makes sense why he referred to me as TG. Hercules must be with them and referring to Paisley as PG so much that it has become tiresome.

Next, I call Lake, and she and Mason are in Toronto. She sounds excited. Apparently, on the night of the dinner, Hercules and Achilles convinced Mason to ease up on working so much. They said they appreciated his loyalty and the blood, sweat, and tears he's given to LTI. And then they offered him a black card, which is a credit card with no limit, and the use of one of their private jets and told him to go wherever he wants in the world for as long as he wants—it's on them.

"They said more to him. I don't know what else they said, but I'm so glad it worked." Then she whispers that she'll get in touch with me when they're back in New York. "Mason's coming." She hangs up.

Before I make a third call to friends, I sit for a moment and think the obvious. For so many years, my perception of the Lord brothers was negatively shaped by Orion. But Hercules and Achilles are indeed good guys. Maybe Orion is, too, somewhere deep down, perhaps.

My third and final call is to Tabatha and James, two friends I haven't seen in forever. They are available for brunch. We meet at MG in DUMBO, which is short for down under the Manhattan Bridge Overpass, since they're already in that neighborhood. MG is a restaurant where one hundred percent of the menu is prepared by molecular gastronomy techniques. And I have a good time with old friends as we catch up, laugh, and plan our next get-together. Of course, they want to meet Achilles. I have a feeling that all my friends are going to want face time with the billionaire known as being elusive and reclusive, and my future husband.

SUNDAY NIGHT

I, surprisingly, have dinner with Caroline. I learned she was in the house working on Friday and Saturday and even this morning. I ran into her in the hallway after discovering I had fresh linens on my bed and my bathroom was spotless. Apparently, she's the one who makes sure all of that happens.

I asked what she was doing tonight for dinner, and she said, "Oh, probably order in."

"Well, have dinner with me!" I said excitedly. "I'd love that. And I'll make bistec encebollado for you."

She laughed delightfully. "How can I say no?"

It has been so pleasant getting to know Caroline. We're eating in Achilles's den and sharing a bottle of red wine.

So far, I've learned that she's single, never married, but she's been in love with a man who has now lived on a tropical island for many years.

I study the beautiful woman carefully. Her looks are almost too distracting, actually. How can someone be that beautiful and display such grace and not be with the man she's been in love with for many years?

"Is that by choice?" I ask, my voice ringing with extreme curiosity.

"Is what by choice?"

"The fact that he's on the island and you're here in the city?" I shrug indifferently. "It's okay, though. I heard that women who are married die younger." I chuckle to let her know that I'm half joking.

"I'm not sure that's true," she says before taking another sip of wine.

My head feels like it's swimming laps without

me. Caroline selected the wine. She said it's one of Achilles's favorite reds. Not only is it delicious, but it's slow in a very decadent way. But I'm pondering Caroline's last comment. I hate generalizing. Generalizing is for those who are too lazy to accept and see the many shades of humanity. And so I say, "I don't think it's completely true. I think a lot of people marry wrong because they marry an illusion. And then they stay in the marriage because it becomes a miserable trap. Those are the ones who die too early. Misery kills." I close my eyes and let the back of my head sink into the couch cushion. "I don't ever want to be miserable."

It's so relaxing, sitting in silence with Caroline, who's a very quiet person. But there's something different about this particular lingering silence, so I raise one heavy eyelid and turn to Caroline.

She's staring at me, lips parted, eyes glossy because they're holding tears.

"Me neither," she whispers. "I don't want to be miserable either."

Very soon after Caroline and I make our declarations to never be miserable, she says she has to leave. She seems very focused on something, but I feel as if I shouldn't ask what's going on inside her head. I'm pretty sure she wouldn't tell if I did ask. So I thank her for having dinner with me and then head to my bedroom.

First, I put on my pajamas, but then I remember tomorrow's Monday, and Achilles specifically said he'll see me on Monday. He hasn't contacted me today. I wonder what he's doing with Paisley and Hercules. I bet it has something to do with TRANSPOT.

I take off my pajamas and slip into my yellow tank dress instead. Then I take that one off and put on a soft pink one—no. I change into my red slip dress. Red is his favorite color. And I want to be ready just in case I run into Achilles in the kitchen tomorrow morning.

Even though I can hardly keep my eyes open, I decide to watch a movie on Netflix, which turns out to be an utter failure. I fall asleep before the first scene ends.

MONDAY MORNING

At first, I hear muted rattling, but the more I rise into consciousness, the clearer the knocking becomes. I take a moment to remember that I'm in bed. Yesterday was Sunday, and today is… Monday!

I sit up quickly. "Who is it?"

"Me, Achilles," he says, sounding muffled behind the thick wood door to my bedroom.

My heart beats a mile a minute from excitement and panic as I look toward the bathroom. "Damn it," I whisper. I wish I could run into the bathroom and brush my teeth, but…

"One second!" I shout and spring out of bed.

I rush to the bathroom and brush my teeth so fast that I might've broken a record.

"Here I come," I call and then rinse my mouth, wipe it with a towel, and splash water over my face to freshen up.

There's no time for a final once-over. I don't know how long that took, but it feels like forever.

I dash back into the room, and facing the door, I steady my heavy breaths while pressing a hand over my racing heart.

"Treasure?" Achilles says.

I turn to the bed. Should I pose on top of it, on my side, and hike up my hip to appear sexier?

"Um…" I deliberate internally.

To hell with it. I dive on top of the bed, and when I'm ready, I say, "Come in."

Yes, You May

TREASURE GROVE

He's in smoky-gray herringbone pants with a silky black polo shirt. I've never known a man who wears clothes as well as Achilles Lord. Sex appeal drips from his rock-hard abs, broad shoulders, and oh gosh, that bulge between his legs.

"It appears you're happy to see me," I say, eyebrows high as I flirt shamelessly.

My eyes shine even brighter watching Achilles toss his head back and his Adam's apple bob as he laughs—a real, hearty, un-Achilles-like laugh.

Then, like a curtain rising to start the performance, his expression slowly transforms. And suddenly, his sultry gaze consumes me as though I'm a delectable dessert and he's famished.

"I'm extremely happy to see you, TG." His words drip from his sexy mouth like honey.

The insides and outside of my body stand at attention. This man, the king of all grumps, who has softened some since we first laid eyes on each other, wants me. And I want him too.

"So…" I whisper seductively. I roll to a kneel.

Achilles's Adam's apple bobs again as he swallows. "You're wearing red."

Smirking flirtatiously, I say, "Just for you," as I slowly raise the bottom of my slip dress up my thighs, revealing succulent flesh. My striptease seems to have put him in a daze as I reveal that I'm not wearing panties.

Achilles mutters a string of undecipherable words. Our gazes stay connected as he lifts his shirt from the hem and then yanks it off over his head with ease. I release a trembling sigh at the sight of his shirtless body. I've always known it existed. I've felt it through his clothes whenever he held me against his *rectus abdominis* , popularly known as his six-pack.

Seeing a man's stomach muscles all fit and pronounced never fails to turn me on. And oh, I am so turned on. His shirt hits the floor, and my dress drops onto the bed almost simultaneously.

"Oh shit," he breathes, his eyes wide as he focuses on my exposed breasts.

So fast, he closes the distance between us while unbuttoning his pants, but he doesn't make it to the zipper. I've moved closer to the edge. And now that he's able to reach me, Achilles has abandoned his zipper to touch me down there.

"Ohm…" I moan, holding onto his arm and biting my lip as his thick fingers slip in and out of me.

"You're so wet," he whispers thickly, stating the obvious.

He stimulates my clit, and I moan as my thighs begin to tremble.

"I've been wanting this for…" He sounds as if he's run out of breath to finish whatever he meant to say. But I know what he was going to say. I've shared the same sentiment.

Our cup runneth over.

The pace of his finger work picks up, and it happens so fast. I'm feverish for more of him. I want those washboard abs on top of me already, so I tug at his zipper—it's down.

Our lips sink against each other's, tongues tangling, and we don't let go as our heads follow his body's motions as he finishes taking off his pants.

They're off.

My fingers are in his hair, holding on to his head, with a large hand against my back, he guides me back down onto the bed. We become a tangle of body parts as we kiss freely, making up for all the hours we wanted to do this but refrained.

"Are you on the pill?" he whispers, and then his tongue drives deeper into my mouth before I'm able to answer.

"IUD," I manage to say as we both take a breath.

His soft and moist mouth is against my ear now, and my head has fallen back against the mattress as his contact sends shivers of delight down my body to my womanhood. My ear is a hot spot, a very hot spot.

"When were you last tested?" he whispers.

Ah… he's so careful, and that's so hot.

"I never fucked Simon without a condom, never," I whisper. And even though I am ready for him to pump deep inside me, I must say, "And I won't let you either."

To my surprise, Achilles chuckles. I thought

what I said might make him cool off, but nope, my words just heated him up. He kisses and nibbles down the side of my face. His silky tongue sensually laps my chin once, twice, three times.

I sough as his tasting of me continues down my neck, my breastbone. I shiver as his tongue plunges into my belly button, making me cry out in sweet delight. Achilles does that again and again.

"Shit, even your belly button tastes delicious, baby," he whispers thickly before his tender tongue takes another dive, but now…

Oh, my…

My thunderous cry of pleasure fills the room as he tongue-bangs my belly button while his fingers stimulate my clit.

As if my senses weren't overloaded enough, his mouth shifts to one side of my waist, where he bites, licks, and tastes my skin, making me and himself moan like crazy. And then his tongue is inside my belly button until his mouth journeys to the other side of my waist and stimulates me just the same.

Achilles moves back and forth across my body like that as an orgasm develops inside me. Overstimulated and ready to burst, I curl my back and lift my hips toward his fingers.

"Yes, baby, come." His voice is deep, dark, and sexy.

I can hardly believe this is happening between us. That it is him who's pleasuring me this way. I'm suddenly thankful that I walked in on Simon and Cherry fucking. If I hadn't, would I have accepted my dad's offer? Would I have signed the contract with Achilles? Would I be right here, right now, mouth open wide, clutching bed linens, choking on air, and…

"Ah!" I cry out as my orgasm spreads deep and intense through my hood.

Then Achilles is up. My body is still on fire. I curl in a ball and lay on my side until the orgasm he ignited continues to subside.

A condom wrapper tears.

I hear him roll the rubber onto his cock.

Oh, his cock. I haven't gotten to touch it or see it yet. And so I look.

I gasp, surprised. Mercy, mercy on me. My jaw drops, and I can't look away from the biggest penis I've ever encountered. It's wide and at least nine inches long.

"It's okay, babe. I'll take it slow." An eyebrow

quirked, he smirks as he strokes the Titanic. He knows he's huge, and he's proud of it.

But I can't close my mouth. "I had no idea," I say, flabbergasted. I know his bulge was healthy, but gosh, his cock is plain obese.

"If you want, we can skip this part and do other things," he says.

Shit, I have to stop staring at it as if I'm afraid of it. I'm not afraid of it.

I swallow the extra moisture that continues to pour into my mouth. "No, I want it," I say like I mean it.

Both his eyebrows quirk up, and now here he comes.

My instincts take over as I roll onto my back. All the hormones that activate during a moment like this, dopamine, endorphins, and oxytocin, have been released. Achilles is between my calves then my thighs. Before he closes the space between us, I slide my fingers down his remarkable abs. Oh my, he's so strong. He has the Titanic in his hand. Our lustful gazes do not detach until…

"Oh G-g-gosh…"

Many Hours Later

We've gone several rounds of full-bodied sex. I feel his heart beating so fast against my back. If he could, I know we would start making love again. But we gave the exercise all we had. My hair is damp. I've been on top of him, riding his cock like a mechanical bull. He's been behind me, pounding me hard and fast, expertly bringing me to a body-quaking, weak-in-the-legs, collapsing-on-the-mattress kind of potent orgasm. Yet and still, I have not had my fill of Achilles Lord. I want more, so much more of him. And I'm certain he wants more of me too. After all, I've just experienced the best sex of my life.

And now, I'm in his arms, our nakedness against each other as my backside is flush with his front side. Achilles has dined on my breasts until he was full, but now he can't take his hands off them. Heck, we can't take our hands off each other.

"Achilles?" I ask, my voice rising in the stillness of the bedroom.

"Yes, TG?"

I chuckle because he's being funny.

"Were you with Hercules and Paisley this weekend?"

He pauses, and I feel him stiffen against me. I wish he hadn't done that. At least I know that he lusts me, but he doesn't trust me, at least not yet. But I don't call him out on it because lust without trust goes both ways.

"Why do you ask?" he says.

Great response. "Because Hercules calls Paisley PG. Therefore, I worked out that wherever you were, you were with them and Hercules constantly referring to Paisley as PG sort of annoyed you." I flip over to face him and, lying on my side, I rest my head in the palm of my hand. Seeing his face again sends a thrill through me. Gosh, he's so gorgeous. That's why I stroke the side of his face until he captures my fingers and kisses the back of my hand. Ooh… the feel of his lips on my skin. I close my eyes to indulge in it.

"So," I say after a long sigh. "I think you were also sort of intrigued by your brother referring to my cousin as PG, and so, in annoyance and adoration, you started calling me TG." I smile playfully.

He tucks two fingers under my chin and then plants a soft soul-rousing kiss on me. "Yet another reason why I can't resist you, TG," he whispers as though my tongue and lips have just taken his breath away.

Eyes still closed as I experience all the good sensations from that kiss, I whisper, "You can't resist me?"

I wait for his response. It's still silent, so I open my eyes to see Achilles grimace in that thoughtful way of his.

"I've tried, but no, I can't resist you," he finally says.

I love his honesty. That's why I follow suit and admit, "Same with me. I've tried but can't."

We stare at each other, and I don't know... it's different this time. It's like we've broken through a gigantic iceberg to become even closer than sex brought us. Then, Achilles guides me against him, and I turn so that my backside is flush against his front yet again.

And as we breathe, we get closer and closer. I bet we would make love again if the Titanic wasn't out of fuel. I have drained it dry.

"By the way, you're good in bed, Mr. Lord," I say.

The breath from his chuckle stimulates the hot spot on my back, and I shiver against him when he says, "So are you."

"Yeah, but you're better. Not all men can make lady parts do what you made mine do. Do you read books or something? You certainly didn't learn those skills by watching porn where every orgasm is a fake orgasm."

The vibration of his laugh against my skin sends more tickling sensations through me.

Achilles kisses my shoulder. "Yes, I was with Herc and Paisley all weekend. My brother's constantly saying PG this or PG that—yeah." He laughs. "It got annoying as hell."

I chuckle. "Those two are quite a pair, aren't they?"

"Indeed."

"Hercules was always the one guy she could never get out of her system. With her it was always, 'But he's not like Hercules Lord,' or 'I wonder if Hercules Lord would do this or that.' And I'd say, 'But Pais, you haven't seen Hercules since high school' or 'since you gave him your virginity in college.'"

"What?" Achilles blurts.

Now I flip over to face him. We smile at each other as our eyes meet. *Do not fall in love, Treasure.*

"Yes, one night of pure serendipity, they ended up at the same party, went back to his place, and Paisley let him have it." I end with a smile because I think it's quite a telling tale, but Achilles appears disturbed by what I said.

"I'm sorry to hear that," he says. "I didn't know that Paisley gave him something pretty precious without believing she'd be able to be with him."

Oh my God—don't, fall, in love.

I tenderly slide my finger across his ruffled eyebrow. "Don't cry for her, Mr. Lord. I lost my virginity the cliche way, in the back seat of my boyfriend's Maserati. Cry for me," I say with a laugh.

Ah, nice… he chuckles. I love it when he chuckles. I kiss his lips, and he kisses me back.

"Can I ask you something?" he whispers, eyes still closed, lips still close to mine after seemingly regrettably ending our kiss.

I narrow an eye. "Sure," I say pensively.

"You've known Orion for many years."

"Mm-hmm," I say, my tone encouraging him to tread lightly.

"Why were you insistent about not doing this with him? And I'm not complaining." The corners of his mouth lift into a sexy smile as his hand glides across the round of my hip to squeeze

him too. After that, we would see each other at pool parties, chat about the old days. He would constantly flirt with his eyes but, while in public, never touch me. Although, his words were penetrative enough.

"It never occurred to me how odd it was that he was keeping his distance when others were around," I say.

"Skylark," Achilles says.

I gasp in awe. "Yes. He was involved with Skylark. How did you know?"

His eyes narrow a pinch. "You said your incident with Orion happened five years ago. It's my job to know who my brothers are involved with."

"Jeez, you said that with a straight face."

His airy chuckle makes me want to kiss him. At some point, we'll have to discuss his tendencies to rival Max Grove in the he's-so-controlling department. However, for the time being, I wonder if I should say more about the day I vowed to never become romantically involved with Orion Lord, ever. Maybe Achilles won't look at me the same after he hears what happened. But I did nothing wrong. On the contrary, I did everything right when the time came to do the right thing. So I summon more courage and continue explaining why his brother puts a sour taste in my mouth.

"Then you know how sweet of a human being she is."

He nods decisively as he clenches his jaw.

Cutting to the chase, I tell him how one night, Orion and I agreed to meet at his villa while everyone else attended a clambake on the beach. I leave out the part about how easy it was for Orion to lure me into bed. We still had a lot of sexual chemistry back then. That night, we pledged our love to each other after taking a trip down memory lane. He had said he missed me and never stopped thinking about me. He was willing to go to the ends of the earth to have me. Then I let him inside me. The sex we had was not even close to being as spiritual, satiating, and gratifying as what I just had with Achilles. If I knew I would one day end up making love with Achilles Lord, then I would've never had sex with a man before him. Today, I was graced with the ultimate sexual experience.

But Orion and I clawed at each other like wild animals, fucking hard. I was on my knees with him behind me, doing the dirty, when Skylark walked in on us. Sweet Skylark with the disposition of a dove stormed into the room and pounded on Orion.

"Then she threw an engagement ring at him." I shake my head, remembering how embarrassed I felt. "Did you know he was engaged to her?"

"He wasn't," Achilles answers.

My jaw drops, and it takes me a moment to process that Achilles hadn't answered my question in the way I thought he would. "You didn't know? I thought…" I thought he knew everything about his brothers. Then I'm struck by illumination. "Of course! Orion was lying to her, playing her, because that's what he does. What the hell is wrong with your brother?"

Now it's Achilles who smashes his forearm over his eyes. "I don't know," he says in a strained whisper.

"Why would he make her think that he's engaged to her if he wasn't going to marry her?" I insist, feeling the same distress I felt back then.

Achilles releases a drawn-out sigh. "He liked Skylark. He really did. But Orion is a saboteur. Do you know how I found the two of you together on my grandfather's island?"

I answer by intensifying my frown.

"He called me and told me where he was and

who he was with as if he was daring me to do something about it."

"Wow" is all I have to say. I pinch my hand over my mouth. That felt like a gut punch and has rendered me speechless.

"I'm sorry, Treasure," Achilles whispers.

His hand stroking my thigh feels so delicious. His touch is wooing me back to our moment, this lovely moment between me and another Lord brother, whom I am contracted to marry.

Jeez… how screwed up is that?

"Where do you see yourself in six years?" I ask Achilles. I know my question isn't fair, but I still want to know what he plans to do with me at the end of all of this.

"I don't know," he says with a sigh. "What about you?"

I flip onto my side, head resting in my palm, to look at him.

His eyes are searching mine too. At this very moment, I want to be with him forever. But is that realistic? We let silence prevail and adjust our mood. We can't let the past or future ruin our present.

Achilles clears his throat and asks, "Are you

still friends with Skylark—assuming that you were friends?"

I nod softly and whisper, "She forgave me." But then I chuckle as I see Skylark and I standing in front of Orion's villa, hashing it out, figuring out who the bad guy is. "We both made a pact to never have anything to do with Orion ever again."

"Ah," he says as if he finally understands why I insisted on not marrying his brother and he approves.

Then we're lost in each other's gazes again. The longer I look into his eyes, the wider my smile becomes. His balmy palm intensifies its squeezing of my flesh. "You're so damn soft," he whispers as if he's touching more the first time

"I want you," I whisper. "I want you inside me now."

I don't have to say it again. Achilles rolls on top of me as my thighs separate to let him in. I hold on to him as our tongues brush, lips quickly joining in. And then, as if it's the most natural thing, I gasp when he slips into my blissful sea.

Date Night

TREASURE GROVE

A chilles and I move to his larger bed. Oh my, I love his room ten times more than mine. First of all, his scent paints the air, and I want to roll around in it and coat myself in it. The decor is so royal and masculine. The prevailing colors are red and gold. I feel so safe with him in this space. And this is where we make love as the night transitions to day. We stopped to eat dinner, though. We ordered sushi from room service. There's not much more erotic than sex and sushi. After we ate, we made out feverishly until he slid himself inside me again. Our love-making has so much depth. When he's inside me, against me, touching me and I'm touching him, my heart feels on the verge of explosion from such exotic emotions. In my head, I say, *I can't love you*, but there's a voice behind that voice that whispers, *It's too late*. I'll ignore those silent words for now.

But after we both climax and are dampened and exhausted from such physical and emotional output, Achilles sets an alarm because neither of us can forsake work for another day, and I fall asleep in his arms.

THERE IS THIS SORT OF ETHEREAL FEEL TO OUR morning sex that makes my head think it's floating to Mars. Achilles tells me it's okay if I continue to sleep in his bed while he dresses for the office. But I let him know he's not the only workaholic in the house.

"I will take a long hot bath before leaving, though," I say, stretching my aching muscles. The exercise of our sex has made me sore all over.

He tugs me into his arms so that our naked bodies are pressed against each other. His skin on my skin, eyes on my eyes, and then lips on my lips reminds me that I am not dreaming, that this is all real.

Gently, softly, our lips part so that we can steady our breaths, and with eyes still hooded, he asks, "How about we have a date night tonight?"

"Yeah," I whisper, still dazed from that kiss. "That'll be great."

ALL DAY AT THE RESTAURANT, EVERYBODY TELLS me how good I look. My skin glows. I'm more smiley. I look well rested.

"You look like you're deeply in love," Lolly says as we sit in our late afternoon meeting to discuss the fallout from canceling all the reservations.

"It's true," Ingrid says, examining me as if I'm a brand-new museum exhibit. "It's hot as hell outside today. The humidity has everybody dragging just to get through, and you're as light as a feather and as fresh as a cream puff."

My laugh is summery. "Food analogies—I like it."

Ingrid and Lolly are mildly amused by my humor, which makes me wonder if I'm too influenced by this new stage I've entered with Achilles. Just as this meeting is about business, Achilles should also be nothing but business mixed with a little—no, a lot—of fun.

"Anyway," I say, scowling at the pages spread out on the table in front of me. "One thing I know, and that's people. We say we're sorry and wish them the best of luck and stay on target to close the event hall next Monday." That was better—that was all business.

I DIDN'T KNOW UNTIL THE LAST MINUTE THAT Achilles had made a reservation at Treasures for the both of us at six thirty. I was in the kitchen with Nya. We had made and were then tasting her new roasted radicchio with bacon, capers, and a walnut cream drizzle. I thought I'd died and gone to heaven when Lauren, tonight's chief hostess, came into the kitchen to tell me that Mr. Lord was waiting for me out front.

"Achilles?" I asked.

"Yes. You have a dinner reservation."

And now I walk into the front and there he is, all panty-melting handsome and wearing his suit better than any other man in the world could.

We smile at each other. I had been waiting all

day to see his face to do what I'm doing now, and that's kiss his lips.

"Dinner, here?" I ask.

Achilles's hands are spread against my lower back, and my arms lie across his shoulders as I pet the back of his neck. "I heard this restaurant has the best food and the sexiest owner in the city." His eyes sparkle a sultry gleam.

Our lips are like magnets resisting the urge to connect. Especially when we both turn simultaneously to see three girls who appear to be in their early twenties walk past us with their camera phones aimed at us.

Achilles looks at them with his famous grimace, but even facing the bull doesn't deter them. It's as if we're not real people to them at all. It's very disturbing.

I feel exposed as Achilles takes my hand, and I turn to Lauren, who says, "Let me show you two to your table."

We're seated in a booth with royal-blue-velour-upholstered cushions. Instead of sitting across from me, Achilles sits beside me.

"Now," he says, our noses nearly touching. "I have you all to myself."

The icky way those girls made me feel dissolves as I smile at him.

"How was your day?" I ask.

"Busy. And yours?"

"Busy."

His lips are a fragment of an inch closer when he says, "I missed you."

Our lips are even closer when I say, "I missed you too."

He licks his lips. They tasted so divine when we kissed out front.

Then I remember something and smirk. "So, should we practice Dr. Brandt's script for public conversation?"

Achilles snorts a chuckle. "I think we're beyond her script, don't you?"

"Yes," I reply, tilting my head curiously. But there are thoughts, or better yet questions, running through my mind that I haven't asked Achilles but want to.

"What is it?" he says, reading my expression.

"Well…" I start but stop when Tom, the head waiter, stands at the edge of our table to take our order.

Like the slow release of gravity, Achilles and I

reluctantly back away from each other so that I can order the seared scallops and he the filet mignon, and then we both agree on a bottle of Mes Fleurs champagne.

Now that we're alone again, that tethering energy draws us close.

"What were you going to say?" he says. I love that he's smiling at me these days more than frowning.

"Oh, yes…" I swallow nervously. I hadn't even given what I want to ask Achilles any thought until this morning as I walked into the foyer of the apartment to ride the elevator down. The front desk had a cab waiting to take me to the restaurant. Ready service along with twenty-four-hour food service almost makes living so high in the sky bearable—almost. "The pen in the glass box— what's up with that?"

Achilles's eyebrows ruffle then reverse. Then he sits very still for a moment, his breathing nearly suspended until he clears his throat.

"It's a pen for Pen—Penelope," he says in a tight voice.

My eyebrows flash up as I feel his pain. "Who's Penelope?"

Achilles purses his kissable lips as though he doesn't want to reveal Penelope's identity. Right away, I know he loves this woman, and because of it, I automatically lean farther away from him.

"Well, what a coincidence," a deep voice says. I rip my attention off Achilles, who quickly turns to see Orion and a very attractive woman, who's not his type at all, actually, standing next to our table.

"Achilles, hello," the woman says as if she's shocked to see him.

Orion's smirk is mischievous, and I know why he looks so naughty when Achilles says, "Pen, Penelope..." and becomes at a loss for words.

WITHOUT BEING INVITED TO SIT, ORION AND THE woman whose presence has been captured in a glass box sitting in Achilles's foyer slide into the opposite side of our booth.

"This is a crazy table we're seated around, isn't it?" Orion says. "Exes all around." He turns to the beautiful woman, who hasn't stopped staring at Achilles with glassy eyes. "Did you know that Treasure is my ex-girlfriend too?"

"I was never your girlfriend?" The words come out breathy, as if they left my mouth without my knowledge.

Achilles hasn't said a word or moved an inch. However, his power scowl has made a big comeback. Finally, he does do something. He puts his hand over mine on top of the table and squeezes.

Suddenly, I release a sigh of relief. He's showing signs of life, signs of who he prefers.

"Sorry to intrude, but when we saw you sitting over here, we couldn't ignore you." Orion sets his penetrating focus on me. "I can never ignore you."

Achilles puts his finger under my chin and kisses me quickly yet tenderly without thought. *Yes!* He's claiming me.

"How did you know we'd be here?" Achilles is glaring at his brother.

Orion shrugs forcefully.

"I'm sorry to intrude," Penelope says.

"It's okay, Pen. I'm sure none of this is your fault."

"But I am glad to see you."

Funny, she hasn't looked at me once. A girl's girl would acknowledge the other woman at the table, especially if she's her ex's new squeeze. I have the feeling she's not as innocent as she claims.

"How have you been? Since I saw you in that awful restaurant a few weeks back?"

"I'm fine." Achilles sounds short. He glances at me. "I was just explaining to TG here"—he smiles a little, and I drop my face bashfully as I snort a soft chuckle—"why I have your pen in a box. Penelope gifted it to me for my birthday." He frowns at her thoughtfully. "What was it? Three or four years ago? We were a couple, but not very many people knew."

"I knew," Orion says.

Penelope's entire face has turned red. Her lips are trembling slightly. I feel her pain. I sense her loss. Achilles is talking about her as if he has no more feelings for her at all.

"The sculptures are Pen's too." He nods graciously at Penelope. "I'll have them packaged and sent to you."

Penelope quickly turns away from Achilles's gaze and then just as quickly looks at him again with a bright smile. "Thank you. I look forward to receiving them. And," she sings, raising a finger, "I'm working with Marigold on the next big charity event. Exciting." Her eyes dance.

"Yes, and, um, your mother is part of the team," Orion adds, smirking at me.

I twist my mouth thoughtfully. Frankly, I don't know how to have any sort of conversation with Orion. Can I ever forgive him for what he did to Skylark and me? It happened a long time ago, but I don't think he's changed a bit.

"You look happy, though," Penelope says directly at Achilles. "Are you happy?" It's as if she's begging him, imploring him, to say no.

"You two are quite cozy, though," Orion chimes in and leans across the table. His face is closer to Achilles. "Don't worry, brother. She knows it's an act. You know, like we talked about earlier today."

My jaw drops as I watch Achilles, who's glaring at Orion like he wants to take his brother by the neck and squeeze.

For some reason, this whole scene gets to me. Tears burn the backs of my eyes. My sinuses swell from sadness. What is this terrible feeling that's building inside me, made of solid sorrow? I drop my face. I've tuned out of this moment. Achilles feels a hundred miles away as Tom comes back with our champagne and asks Orion and Penelope if he should take their orders.

"No," Achilles says in a firm voice that dares anyone to challenge him. "They're getting up and going, right now."

Achilles and Orion have a stare off that's filled with violence. It's as if at any second, they will come to blows.

Then, Orion sucks his teeth and bounds quickly to his feet. He walks away without checking to see whether Penelope is behind him.

"I'll see you soon, Achilles," she says, sliding out of the booth. "You're still on the charity's board, aren't you?"

After glaring at her for several beats, Achilles nods sharply and then says, "Good night, Penelope."

And still, Penelope doesn't look at me. She doesn't say good night to me, but she says it to Achilles, except her "good night" actually sounds like "I love you."

IT FEELS AS IF THEY'VE RUINED OUR NIGHT. TOM wanted to pour our wine, but Achilles ordered him to leave it. He'll pour it. And so he filled my glass three-quarters of the way and then his. I haven't been able to move a muscle. My body has been rendered immobile by Orion and Penelope, who reminded me that my relationship is fake and that I know for certain that I shouldn't trust the man who has taken me to sexual galaxies that I never knew existed.

"I was going to marry her," he says.

I close my eyes and allow the sting of his words to jolt through me.

"And I did love her. But she broke up with me."

I open my eyes and stare at the blue velvet cushion of the seat in front of me, although the fibers and color are out of focus. Oh, the pain… I'm working to get past it. I'm trying to swim past all the emotions that almost made me fall in love with Achilles Lord so that I can stand on the shores of pragmatism and self-preservation.

"It hurt for a long time," he continues. "I couldn't be with her because I had to make sure Hercules married a fifth cousin named Rain first. It was the only way we could receive the financial benefit of the trust.

"But Herc married Paisley. He would've given

it all up for her. Treasure?" he whispers, and his voice is thick with emotion.

After taking one deep breath to be able to bear looking at his face without feeling love, I turn toward him. My heart swells with an emotion that I don't want right now.

"I was never willing to give it all up for her. But I would do it for you." He nods softly. "I just would."

I don't nod. I don't smile. I don't move a muscle. Because frankly, I don't trust him.

"And Orion lied. I never had a discussion with him today. And I wonder how the hell he found out we were having dinner here." I see anger in his eyes.

I actually believe him.

"You gotta believe me, Treasure." His eyes plead with me.

I nod softly and then whisper, "I believe you."

He takes me by the hand, and God help me, I can't stop myself from enfolding my fingers with his. Because here's the truth—I'm still swimming in that sea of love when it comes to Achilles, and I can't even see the shore of reason and self-preservation from here.

"Let's get out of here," he says and grabs the

champagne by the neck. "And take this with us. I want to show you what I've been up to all day. Then you'll know nothing about how I feel about you is an act."

My eyes can no longer contain the tears that slip down the side of my face. Achilles brushes the tears from my cheeks, caresses my chin as his thumb slides sensually across my bottom lip, and then our mouths melt into each other's.

———————

TOM HAD OUR DINNER PACKED TO GO. OUR MEALS smell divine as Dan drives us in a direction nowhere near Achilles's penthouse. Achilles hasn't let my hand go as we sit in the back seat of the car. I hate that Orion showed up with a plan to ruin our night and basically succeeded. I mean, why would he say that Achilles admitted to him that he was faking it with me? Maybe Orion knows about our session with Dr. Brandt. Of course, that's it.

"A million for your thoughts," Achilles says.

Gosh, I've been lost in thought, gazing unfocused at the back of the front passenger's seat.

But I smile reassuringly at Achilles and say, "I'm thinking, what a crash-and-burn night."

He grunts a soft chuckle, and then his sexy lips land in a smirk. "You know what I'm thinking?"

Mesmerized by his nearness, I shake my head.

"I'm thinking…" His eyebrows furrow, and his lips look to be stuck at the beginning of whatever he wanted to say. Achilles clears his thought. "I'm thinking this night hasn't crashed or burned because I'm with you." He raises my hand to his lips and kisses the backs of my knuckles.

I have a feeling those weren't his initial words, but I'll take the second option too.

"Why are we on East Sixty-Ninth?" I ask now that I'm paying attention to our surroundings.

The antiquated neighborhood is gorgeous. It's near the park and where all the old three-story townhomes reside. My parents have a place not far away.

"Remember when I said that I hear you?" Achilles asks as the car comes to a stop in front of a gorgeous white stone townhome with lane windows and all the trimmings of an early-twenti-eth-century abode including wrought-iron balconies, bulging seat windows, and grand front steps fit for royalty.

I'm trying to work out what this all means in my brain.

"This isn't…" I rip my eyes off the gorgeous townhome. "Do you…?"

I love his smile—gosh, I love it.

"Is this close enough to the ground for you?"

Top Rag Mag

66 Hold on to your lattes, people, because it has just been confirmed that Achilles Lord and Treasure Grove have been seen in public, kissing and canoodling, and, well… it was hot.

Check out the photos below.

They are indeed a couple of true lovebirds.

Comment below.

Getting Cozy

TREASURE GROVE

Achilles is inside me, filling me up with his engorged cock. Everything has changed since we moved into the townhouse. We make love often in the bed we share in the room we share. Whenever Achilles is inside me, I feel so completely in love with him.

Today is the end of the second week that we've lived in the townhome. We've fallen into routines that prove Achilles and I may have been destined to live together. For instance, we wake up at the same time every morning and cook breakfast, eat, and put the dishes in the dishwasher together. I concede that Achilles cannot live without a real housekeeping crew, and frankly, neither can I, because we are two very busy people. I bring dinner home from the restaurant on most nights.

Almost every day in the last two weeks, Achilles has stopped by the restaurant. Usually, his reason is common sense when he enters my office, locks the door, bends me over my desk, and his magnificently large cock thrusts into my dripping wetness from behind. Once our burning and unquenchable lust for each other has been quelled for the moment, Achilles and I will get right down to business. He's helping with the structural changes of the restaurant. The cost of construction is half as much of what I was initially quoted. Achilles is making sure I'm not getting taken advantage of in any way.

I go to his office often too. I never really understood why he needs the deal between my family and his family to work until now. He showed me hundreds of pages of trust requirements for the Lords to abide by. We've had deep conversations about why a man would do something like that, make his descendants jump through hoops from the grave. Achilles and I can talk for hours about stuff like that with our clothes on or off. He's a good guy—a really good guy. And for now, he's mine.

But today is Sunday, the second Sunday in our new place and the second weekend we've spent in bed, reading the papers, talking about business decisions that have boded well or need more tweaking, and making lots of love. I am, for all intents and purposes, being extremely negligent when it comes to protecting my heart. Because nothing has changed as we lie in bed, limbs entangled, after engaging in beautiful sex. My heart pumps fast, our bodies glisten, my soul is full of Achilles Lord, and still, we are connected by our signatures on the dotted line of a contract.

"Guess what?" he whispers against the sensitive spot on the back of my shoulder that sends shivers of delight to my lady parts.

"Yes?" I sigh. *Mmm… that felt so good.*

Achilles chuckles. He knows exactly what he just did to me. "On Wednesday, we'll be officially married."

The shock of what he revealed makes me gasp and flip over to face him. "Has it been four weeks already?"

"It has," he says, gazing at my face as if the sight fills his heart with joy. Achilles looks at me this way a lot.

"Time sure has flown by," I say softly, taking in every inch of his face too.

He trails his fingertip from one side of my nose to the other. "I'm going to run off with your freckles and make them my mistress."

I touch his dimpled chin and the dimple on his right cheek. "I'm going to elope with these, and we'll engage forever in a ménage à trois."

Achilles graces me with a sultry chuckle as he reaches over my hip to squeeze my ass and then guides me under him. "Don't forget, we have dinner with my brother and PG in less than an hour," he says, and then we both moan in unison when he moves inside me.

ACHILLES LORD

"The two of you are pretty cozy," Herc says.

It's after dinner. Herc and I have taken our conversation into his den while TG and PG scurried off to PG's office so that TG can show her some of the culinary schools she's considering applying to. I glare toward Paisley's den. Maybe at some point, this insatiable need to have her, be inside her, and put my hands on every part of her body, especially her ass—*Damn, her ass*—will pass, but tonight, I still want her all the time. I don't know, maybe this is what being in love is all about. I've never been in love… until now.

"Yeah," I say with a longing sigh.

During dinner, Treasure and Paisley mostly reminisced about the past, recounting stories of how they caused trouble together. Treasure is definitely the naughty one of the two.

Damn…

When my cock is absorbed by her warmth and wetness, it feels like heaven on earth, but being satisfied with Treasure goes beyond sex. She's smart as a whip. She's rational about subjects such as politics, business, and psychology. Emotional intelligence—she's replete with emotional intelligence which actually makes her a formidable foe and ally. She'll officially become my wife on Wednesday. I don't know how I feel about it. I don't think I like it.

I turn my frown onto my brother because he's working in concert with his wife. I could see the concern on Paisley's face when the conversation took a turn from Heartly Rose Grove, Paisley's mother, still being upset that she and Herc eloped to Treasure announcing that I convinced her to enroll in culinary school.

"You were able to persuade her," Paisley said, looking at me with one eye askew.

Then Treasure said that she's gained three love pounds since we've been living together, and then she put her hand on my cock, which was already hard, and rubbed as she said, "And he's gained five."

Treasure's into getting me all hot and bothered in public places so that I can excuse myself and she can excuse herself as we find a quiet hiding place to fuck it out.

That's why I can't look toward Paisley's den. Not long after Treasure rubbed my cock, Paisley made sure to separate us.

I picked up on something while we were at LTI's undisclosed lab in the Bahama's. Paisley and Herc know how to communicate their displeasures telepathically. I gather he and I are in his den drinking bourbon because she wants him to get a read on me. She's worried that I'll leave Treasure high and dry and broken hearted. That'll never be my intention. But still, if I'm not mistaken, Hercules is taking a tone with me, and I don't like it because he should know better than to see me the way she does.

"What about Pen?" Hercules asks.

"What about her?" I bite back.

Hercules steadily holds my gaze.

"What the fuck is this interrogation for? I've been living with Treasure for a month, Herc. She didn't feel comfortable living in the penthouse, so I bought her a thirty-five-million-dollar town-home. I make love to her every day, multiple times a day. So don't ask me about Pen."

Hercules remains as steady as an iceberg as he folds his arms over his chest. "Do you love her?"

Say it.

My lips won't move.

Say it, goddamn it.

TREASURE GROVE

"So…" Paisley says as if she's singing a note in a pop song. "It's getting pretty hot and heavy between you and Achilles."

I've just showed her the school that's my first

choice. There's a reason why I've been avoiding Paisley ever since Achilles and I went full-on sex. But Achilles agreed to have dinner with them without checking with me first. He thought it was time we come up for air, and I sort of agreed. However, I would've chosen a different set of friends to sit down and eat with than my overprotective cousin and her husband. That's the nature of our relationship—she looks out for me, and I look out for her. But I've sensed Paisley's discomfort about how close Achilles and I have grown ever since I said the word "love pounds." I didn't mean to use the L word. It just slipped out. Achilles didn't cringe from the word. And when I rolled my hand up and down his cock, he was still hard after I said it.

"We have sex," I come right out and say. Paisley has never known me to beat around the bush, and so I won't start now. "Loads of it." Actually, we should be banging right now.

Paisley is very quiet as we both stare at the computer screen. The longer we sit in silence, the more I know she's waiting me out. It might not look like it, but we are indeed communicating.

"I'm protecting my heart," I assure her.

"Because," Paisley says as she whips my swivel chair around so I can face her. Her eyes are filled with so much emotion. "Because, Treas, I love Hercules so much that I ache if I think about ever losing him. But my blood is your blood…"

"And your heart is my heart," we say together.

We smile at each other as love fills me, and I'm certain her love for me is filling her to the brim too.

Then she sighs. "It's just that Achilles is all business, all the time. And he won't talk to me or Hercules about how he feels about you."

I sit up straight, absorbing what she just revealed.

"Why do you think that is?" I strain to say. It feels as if my head is floating away from my body. Perhaps, finally, the truth is ready to sit on my shoulders like a two-ton elephant.

"Truth?" she asks.

I'm only barely able to perceive that I am nodding.

Paisley frowns as she looks down, unfocused. "I don't know." Her eyes are back on mine. "But you know my dad and your dad."

My shoulders slump as I sigh. "Yes, I do." And I've been trying to think about whatever shit they're up to.

"The double cross is coming," she says. "And you know it."

My chest feels heavy, and suddenly, the thought of being happy forever with Achilles Lord seems like a fantasy. "I know it," I whisper.

The Double Cross

ACHILLES LORD

BRIGHT AND EARLY

Her body is so damn soft. I ache to feel her against me. Her hair carries the scent of orange blossoms, and her skin is like silk, supple against my touch and squeeze. It's morning. Soon, my alarm will sound, and when that happens, I won't have a minute to spare for this.

I steer my cock against her perfect round and firm ass. Treasure breathes, stirs, and pushes closer against me. Good, baby. Wake up and come to daddy.

I roll my tongue around that spot on her

shoulder that always makes her hot. "Mmm…" My cock grinds between her ass again. But I better watch out, because if I keep grinding her, I will blow.

She sighs and whispers, "Mmm, Achilles."

I stroke down the side of her body, the curve of her waist, to her belly, and then my mouth waters when I slide my fingers into her moisture —she's dripping wet.

Treasure moans and squirms against me.

Yes. I have her full cooperation.

I rub her clit, and she wriggles some more, clutching the pillow. *More.* She rides against me, whimpers. *More.* Shit… I would rather be tasting her, doing this with my tongue, but it's too late. I should've started with my tongue. I am arriving closer to blowing. She needs to come fast. *More.* My beautiful woman cries out, and I press up against her, slip as many fingers as I can inside her and… sigh… I feel her walls pulse around me. Shit. What a beautiful thing, when a woman's sex throbs as she orgasms. *More.* I hurry up and glide inside her, filling her, stretching her. She's so damn warm—no, she's hot, balmy, inviting.

"Shit…" I moan. Each plunge and pull brings me closer.

More. I can't yet, though. I want to feel her pulsing around my cock. *More.* In and out, I work her clit. Fuck. *You can do it, Achilles. Don't. Come. Yet.*

"Oh Achilles, please," she cries in pleasure.

Yes, baby. Like that.

Her sighs are deep, hard, and then her head falls against my collarbone. Her ass tightens. Her walls quake around me, and it feels so damn…

"Oh, shit!" I release myself inside her.

TWO HOURS LATER

Treasure is in the kitchen. She's wearing my favorite red slip and a matching silk robe. I'm suited up. I can't get started with her yet again. I went down on her after she showered. My tongue rubbing her clit, I watched her fingers dig into the comforter, felt her hips ride my mouth and then retract when I brought her closer to climax. She came, and I finished inside her. Twice in one morning is not enough for us, but it should get me through the day. I can't do it again. My cock is too sore. Treasure gave me this healing ointment to put on it. But last night, when we made it home from Herc's place, how many times did we fuck? Two? Three? It was three. I winced when I put on my pants. The healing ointment will make me ready for her tonight. But not now. The salve needs time to work its magic.

"I made banana crepes," she says, holding a forkful in front of my mouth for me to taste. One hand on her back, I guide her closer, and I take the bite of food.

"Mmm," I say, closing my eyes, letting them fall to the back of my head. I'm not patronizing her when I say that she's a fantastic cook. She's just as good as Barbara. "That's delicious, baby."

Her eyes always narrow just a fragment when I call her "baby." I've been meaning to ask her why. But then, why ask why when I already know the answer?

This is getting real between us—very real. It's almost time to ask her what we are going to do about that contract.

"Sit. Eat with me, if you have time," she says, her beautiful face beaming at me. My own personal morning sun.

I don't have time. I'll be late for a meeting with John, my accountant. "Yeah, I have time."

I listen to her talk about a lunch she had with

her mother on Tuesday of last week. She already mentioned the lunch on Tuesday night. However, this morning, details are different. She says that her mother and aunt have become friends with my mother, Marigold. She thinks my mother's new role is Heartly and Londyn Grove's referee. However, her mother and my mother hit it off the most. They're thinking about planning more events together. She's about to say more—I can see it in her eyes—but instead, she smiles pensively.

"Achilles?" she says.

I raise my eyebrows. *Humph?*

Her lips are parted. We do this a lot—want to say something to each other but stop short of getting it out

"I'm falling in love with you. And I'm scared," she bravely admits.

My chest is tight as I search her watery eyes for signs of deception. I see no signs of deception. But I've been waiting weeks to hear her say something like that. Now that I've heard it, my sore cock wants to rise. It wants her warmth, her wetness.

I scowl at my watch. "Can we talk about this

when we get home later? Six," I say, gazing into her confounded eyes. "Be home at six."

Her tongue presses against her top teeth as if she wants to say something.

I wish we were standing so that I could bring her into my arms, kiss her soft lips. "I want to address this, what's happening between us, but not on the go. And, um…" I raise an eyebrow. "I'm going to need the healing ointment to work its magic too."

Smiling gently and blushing, she looks down and nods.

I've got to get the hell out of here before I make love to her and be *really* late for my meeting with John.

I stand. "Six o'clock on the dot?"

Still smiling, she says, "Six o'clock on the dot."

NOON

This has been the difficult part of my day, concentrating on work and not Treasure. She's become an addiction. Her sweet honey pussy has become like breath to me. Her voice, her laugh, the way she consumes every word I speak when she's seeking my knowledge about business—that all makes me want to be in her presence every minute of the day. But that's impossible. I never felt this way about Pen. I never knew feeling this way was possible, at least not for me. Pen was convenience. My connection to her was practical. A man needs a woman, a wife, heirs, so he finds someone who's good on paper. But Treasure is good on paper, in my bed, in my space, and in my soul.

She's falling in love with me?

She's not already in love with me?

All of a sudden, Nero bursts into my office. The force of his steps and the way he's grabbing at the air makes me rise to my feet.

"What is it?" I ask.

"Those fuckers!" he shouts and then balls his fist and bites his knuckle.

"Which fuckers?" Nero knows I'm not one to play guessing games.

"The Groves."

He starts talking, and suddenly, my happy house of cards comes crashing down.

TREASURE GROVE

Construction on the integration is moving along like a fine-tuned machine. Today was the day that I assessed the moving parts of the restaurant. Achilles said that my job was to make sure the process of running the outfit is smooth, consistent, and profitable. Once those three components are in place, then Treasures will become an asset, and I can easily step away from the daily operations to pursue my true hope and dream, which is to become a head chef. I'm so frightened to abandon scratching for every dime, trying to find success around every corner, but I'm so ready for it. If not now, then when?

I just left my operations team. The new storage shelves are being installed at this very moment. I race to my office to fetch my cell phone so that I can send a photo of the shelves already up and running to Achilles since he was the one who suggested them. But when I take my cell phone out of the top drawer of my desk, I notice three messages from my dad.

My organs feel as though they're tying in knots as I call him back. Leo never calls me that many times if the subject matter isn't important. He answers on the first ring.

"Dad?" I say, hoping nothing's actually wrong but knowing the opposite is true. I feel it has something to do with Achilles too. The moment I've hoped would never arrive I'm sure has come.

"Treasure Chest, have you heard?"

My frown is so intense that my head hurts. "Heard what?"

"Great. I didn't want you to hear this from anyone but me."

"Hear what?" My tone is sharp enough to cut steel.

"You are no longer obligated to marry Achilles Lord. Your contract has been nullified."

"What?" I cry, feeling distressed.

He said that they were able to cut the same deal made with the Lords with another powerful family, the Christmases. He says it's a cleaner bargain that doesn't include marrying off his only daughter to a man like Achilles Lord.

"But I love Achilles!" I shout, feeling as if I'm tumbling downhill at full speed. "What have you done, Dad? What have you done?"

My phone beeps that I have another call. It must be him, Achilles. I have to explain that I had nothing to do with my dad's handling of this whole ordeal. So I switch over the call without even saying goodbye to my dad, whom at this very moment, I don't know if I can ever forgive.

But then I look more carefully at the screen. The caller is not Achilles—it's someone else.

I'm For Real

TREASURE GROVE

The caller was Paisley, and she said that Lake is at the hospital and shouldn't be alone. Luckily, they were in the city for three days before traveling to Sydney, Australia, when it happened.

I take a cab to the Presbyterian Hospital. On the way, I call Achilles a number of times, but it continually goes straight to voicemail. He knows what my family has done. He hates me and every Grove on the planet. Even my mom might lose Marigold as a best friend. My dad, who takes what he wants and does what he wants without considering the fallout, has ruined my happiness.

And I'm numb, so numb that all I can do is stare, dazed, out the windshield from the back seat. All day long, I've been walking as if dancing on air. I knew that tonight would've been the start of something new between me and Achilles.

"I would marry him for real," I whisper in a shaky voice. Then I close my eyes to stop the tears from pouring out.

But we don't have five years sealing us together anymore. Am I ready to be married now? I'm not sure of it.

I massage my temples but only long enough for Lake to call me and ask if I'm on my way. I tell her I am, and she breaks down in a gut-wrenching sob, leaving me shouting, "Is Paisley there?" over and over again.

I thought Paisley was already at the hospital.

Of course she isn't there. She, like me, has found out that her father betrayed her husband's family.

I MAKE IT TO THE HOSPITAL AND THEN WALK SO fast that I'm nearly running into the building. I've stopped worrying about my relationship with Achilles, and my complete focus is on making sure I make it to Lake so that she won't feel so alone.

The front desk tells me that Mason is being treated in a private ICU wing. I imagine LTI is paying for his hospital stay. I'm given access to a special hallway and elevator, and after a short ride, I hurry out of the elevator, down a sterilized hallway, and into a private waiting room where Lake is sitting in a chair bent over, sobbing into her hands.

"Lake?" I say tentatively.

She whips her head up and gazes at me as if I'm an apparition. "It's too soon," she whimpers. Tears stream down her face like a rapidly flowing river.

She's on her feet, and I'm closing the distance until we are hugging each other so tight I feel like it's best to never let her go.

But many minutes later, I do let her go. Lake is obviously done for. Mason is on life support. They're not married, so she's waiting for his parents and sister to arrive. She doesn't want them to take him off life support.

"I believe in miracles," she keeps saying.

I repeatedly let her know that I do too. And

I'm not bullshitting. I truly believe in miracles. It's one of many lessons that my grandfather taught us. He used to say that believing in miracles helps us dream. It helps us find the answers to the impossible questions.

Then I go right to work for her, calling Lake's parents and her cousin, the bossy one named Amy, who drops everything and says she'll be arriving tonight.

Two hours in, and a nurse informs Lake that she can sit by Mason's side. She gets out of her seat so fast that she generates a mild wind. Now that she's gone and many people will soon arrive, I call my restaurant and have catering set up a buffet-style dinner in the waiting room for visitors and hospital staff.

I have to keep myself busy or else I'll remember my own grief. So I arrange and pay for flights for Lake's family and then arrange ground transportation from the airport to the hospital. I reserve hotel rooms for them near the hospital since I'm certain Lake will not be returning home until Mason is able to leave this hospital with her.

"He'll recover," I whisper to myself, and that's when they walk out of the elevator—Paisley,

Hercules and—my heart constricts and jaw drops —Achilles.

ACHILLES AND I LOCK EYES. EVEN AS I HUG Paisley and then Hercules, I'm unable to look away from him.

"I can't believe this," Paisley says. We're hugging again.

Hercules goes to the nurses' station, and Achilles rips his gaze off me to join his brother. I'm not quite sure if Achilles is upset at me or not. He doesn't look mad or disheveled or defeated. Maybe he's done playing the game of pretending he's in love with me at all. I too felt that pinch, that very tiny pinch, of freedom when my dad told me that I'm no longer beholden to that contract. I assume I'm able to keep the money. I better be able to keep the money.

"I know," I say, comforting Paisley by rubbing her back.

"He's in a coma?" She detaches from me to shake her head. "I can't believe that."

"Babe, let's go," Hercules says to Paisley.

She nods, and I watch as she closes the

distance between them, he so naturally curls an arm around her back, and they shuffle together down the same hallway Lake disappeared through.

And now, I'm staring into his eyes again. My breaths are so deep that my chest rises high and drops low.

"Can we talk?" he asks.

Of course, I nod.

I follow Achilles to a door that beeps and then opens. That's what he was doing at the nurses' station, arranging privacy for us. We go down a brightly lit corridor. Every so often, he turns back to look at me. There's so much we have to say to each other. Maybe our time together ends here and now. The thought makes my heart actually ache.

Finally, he leads us into an empty hospital room. His familiar scent makes my head spin. I still love being near him.

Maybe I should say something first. "So," I say.

"I was…" he says at the same time.

I press my lips together to smile and swallow. "You first."

He nods stiffly. We both know that it's best if he goes first.

"I don't hold what your father, uncle, and brother did against you."

I don't know what to say or do. I'm immovable because I can feel that he's about to lower the boom.

His famous scowl intensifies as he stares into my watery eyes. I can no longer keep the tears I've been keeping myself from shedding over him tucked away. They're rolling down my cheeks.

I'm shocked and relieved when Achilles wraps his arms around my waist and guides me to him. The way we're standing with each other is a promising sign. The silence urges us to do more, though. The way we're staring into each other's eyes makes my breaths short and sharp.

"I'm sorry," I finally chirp.

Achilles gently swipes tears from one side of my face and then the other. "You warned me. Remember?"

I nod softly and then close my eyes. "I hoped they wouldn't, though."

Suddenly, his lips are on mine, his tongue in my mouth, and our kiss so delicate and needy that I'm floating in his arms.

"I love you, Treasure Grove," he whispers before his tongue dips back into my mouth.

"I love you too," I whisper between kisses.

Then—it happens so suddenly—Achilles drops to one knee, and I'm staring at a gorgeous princess-cut diamond ring.

"Then let's make it official. Let's make it for real. Marry me—one day." He's displaying my favorite smirk.

"Yes," I say strongly through my own happy smile. I want him to have no doubt that I mean it when I say, "Yes, I'll marry you—one day."

Achilles takes my hand and slides the ring on my finger.

"We'll keep what we have going?" he asks.

I nod ardently. "Absolutely."

Achilles and I press our foreheads together and stand this way, eyes closed, as the seconds tick by.

"How are you doing?" I finally ask, feeling that this moment between us is truly bittersweet.

"Better now that I've taken care of this part. But…" he sighs heavily. "Mason had his whole life ahead of him. Just when he found the woman he loves, he gets hit with this. It doesn't seem fair."

"I know," I sigh.

We stand comfortably in stillness and silence for a little while longer. His nearness is starting to get the better of me, and we both turn to look at the empty hospital bed at the same time.

"Not now?" he asks.

"Um, hashtag inappropriate."

We chuckle together.

"But," I say as I unbuckle his belt and unzip his pants. "It's never too inappropriate for a BJ."

Achilles's eyebrows shoot up as I go down on him and take his big cock into my mouth and taste him, lick him, and suck him until he quakes with an orgasm, and then I drink every drop of him.

Mason Vayle Harper — Time of death 11:23:05 p.m.

Recompense

ACHILLES LORD

NINE DAYS LATER

The last nine days have been hectic, to say the least. I couldn't have gotten through them without the woman sitting to my left, TG.

Mason's death hit us all hard, but not as hard as it hit his fiancée and Hercules. But he, we, couldn't let us lose ground. I reminded Herc that nobody wanted this moment to occur more than Mason. He was so important to our operation, to our progress, that he owned five percent of stock in LTI, and he had been wise enough to officially transfer his holdings to Lake Mary Clark, who has handed over her vote to PG.

I'm certain Max, Leo, and Xander saw this coming. On the night I proposed to Treasure, and after Mason died, she and I returned to our townhome and sat on the rooftop and drank a bottle of wine in silence. For a long time, Treasure sat next to me on the chaise lounge, head on my chest, I smelling her hair and she listening to my heart.

The sun poked through the eastern horizon when she finally asked, "Now, what do we do about my family?"

And since then, we've been steadily heading toward this moment.

Treasure and I are already seated. In walks Max Grove, Xander Grove, and Leo Grove who's not happy to see her and me sitting so close. Paisley and Herc stand at the head of the table. We're in the executive conference room at LTI.

I keep my eyes on Max Grove. It was Treasure who insisted that we add Lake's name to the list of investors even if the shares hadn't finished being transferred to her name. Slouching in his chair, he seems to have a chip on his shoulder as he reads the top sheet and then stiffens. Treasure squeezes my thigh under the table. Hell if she wasn't right. Max Grove is going to be easier to deal with during this negotiation from here on out. He even looks up and down the table as if searching for Lake's ghost. There's no way we expected her to be here. Even though she knows her name will be invoked to influence Max.

"Monitors up," Paisley says into the table microphone. Three large-screen monitors power on. Then Paisley's mother's face appears on one monitor, and Xander nearly jerks himself out of his seat.

"Heart?" he says and frowns at Paisley. "What's your mother doing here?"

Paisley repeats GIT's rule on owners' voting rights to override the CEO's decision.

"Today is that day, Dad," she says. "But you're going to want to see this first."

"We're all present. Let's get started," Hercules says.

It's so quiet we could hear a mouse scuttle across the floor. The lights come down as a large screen lowers against the wall. And the video plays of TRANSPOT actually working. I remember when I saw the demonstration in real life. I was fucking blown away.

Five individuals from five corners of the world in one room as solid digitized images of them-selves having tangible forms. Each image could interact with the others—they shook hands and patted each other on the back. At this stage in development, their interactions were minimal, but the possibilities are endless.

The video ends. The lights are up. Xander, Leo, and Max are three pictures of shock, but Max displays rage too.

"It works," Max growls, aiming his death stare at Paisley who nods stiffly.

"I, who've never"—Max slams his fist on the table—"crossed you…"

The door opens, and Bethel, one of the administrative assistants, escorts Lake into the room.

"Sorry I'm late," she says. "I thought maybe I should be here for…" Her words trail off as she looks at Max's face.

Yes.

Max sits up straight, zips his lips, and tries hard not to look in Lake's direction as she takes a seat beside Treasure.

Feeling the victory, I wink at her. It was brave of her to show up.

"So, Dad, Uncle Leo, it works," Paisley says.

"What you did was illegal," Leo says.

"You were never going to get it to work

without me." Paisley taps the tip of her finger to the side of her head. "The know-how is up here. Because Grandfather told me everything he knew about the light sources that can collect and solidify molecular particles and a brilliant team of scientists, programmers, Hercules, and myself figured out how to bring it to life."

"Damn it, Paisley, how could you?" Xan mutters, shaking his head and glaring at her as if he's disappointed in her. He sounds defeated on one hand but there's a hint of something else in his voice too.

But if there's one thing I've learned about Paisley, it is that she is a champ at keeping her emotions in check. She already knows her father, uncle, and brother inside out. She even said that at first, just to be loyal to the fight they've been carrying on with my family for years, they'll buck and kick, but they'll be in from the moment the video ends.

"Let's just vote already," Treasure says. "We need more than fifty-fifty. I have Lynx's proxy. We're a full vote together." She smiles devilishly, and I want to plant a sensual kiss on her sexy mouth. "We say, 'Yea.'"

Max glares at her with pinched eyes. I want to

laugh out loud, but that wouldn't be appropriate or smart.

"The moms?" Treasure calls.

"Yea," Heartly and Londyn say in unison.

"Yea. That's three," Paisley says and beams in on her father. "Dad. It's TRANSPOT, and it works. Fifty-fifty full rights ownership, LTI and GIT. And remember that I, your daughter, am half owner of LTI."

Silence lingers as Xander and Leo stare at each other, somehow having a full conversation as their expressions move through several variations.

"No," Max says and sets his jaw, refusing to look in Lake's direction.

However, it's always favorable when Xander and Leo speak to each other with their eyes.

"What about the trust deal?" Leo asks me.

I beam in on him. It takes everything I have to not call him a snake from hell. But in this instance, we have the upper hand, and our advantage is solid. I made sure of it. The only way they're able to cut us out is if they sue Paisley. That's why today, after this vote, if either Leo or Xander sides with us—because that's what it will take to break a tie—then the agreement will be signed, filed, and made a legal and binding document.

"Dad," Treasure says, smiling at him with her eyes. "My future husband and I will forgive you for your snaky ways if you say yes."

I'm surprised that Leo is grinning at her when he nods and says, "It's a 'Yea' from me."

"Me too." Xan looks down as if he knows he's about to crush his son, raises two fingers, and says, "Yea."

The sound of Max leaping to his feet and then storming out of the room steals everybody's attention.

But as soon as he leaves, Nero comes in, the agreements are signed, handshakes commence, and champagne is poured.

FIVE HOURS LATER

TREASURE GROVE

It's late, and we're drunk because surprisingly, when the Groves and Lords get together for a real party, it's on fire. After we signed the contracts,

Marigold revealed that she was with my mom and Heart, who were at Heart's apartment in the city. They invited us over for proper celebratory cocktails. Hugo and Leslie showed up. Music was played. There was dancing. And my man has been stuck with an engorged cock ever since our first slow dance. Finally, it's time to relieve him.

Epilogue

ORION LORD

ONE YEAR LATER

T tried calling Lilah, but she won't answer her phone. Fuck. And now I'm at the office on a Saturday morning. Achilles is in Las Vegas, preparing for his cheesy, cheap-ass wedding to *her*. I would have never given a woman of *her* caliber that kind of a cliché wedding. I wouldn't care if she asked for it. She still wouldn't get it.

Anyway, Herc is in Vegas too. Everybody's in Vegas except me. That's why I've been calling Lilah nonstop. I need her to work this weekend, with me, as my date. I think it's a good deal—a date in Vegas with me and…

"Orion," Cab, one of the tech guys, says as he enters my office and tells me, using computer jargon, what went wrong with the servers.

I rise from sitting on the edge of my desk. This is almost over. I have a date tonight with Penny or Patricia. As far as the wedding goes, I asked Penelope if she wanted to be my date, but she told me to go to hell and hung up in my face. Ever since the night we crashed Achilles's and *her* date, Pen's been blowing dragon fire at me.

I lied to her—okay. I sent her flowers and an apology that I really meant. Well… Lilah sent the flowers and wrote the apology.

Where the hell is she?

I point at Lilah's computer sitting on top of her desk outside my office. "I just need to get into that computer over there."

Cab grins as if he's the happiest guy in the world. "Go for it. It's all up and running."

I will know exactly who I have a date with tonight once I'm on Lilah's computer. She worked late last night, and the computers went down before she was able to push my updated calendar to my server.

"Should I stand by just in case there's a problem?" Cab asks.

"Sure," I say. Why not.

I type in *YYYHMAHLE123*. That's her password. I know it because she wrote it on a sticky that I confiscated.

But for some reason, I'm reading her password differently today. *Why him?*

I'm in, and a Word document pops up.

It's a…

> *Dear Orion Lord, (You fucking narcissist— remember to delete)*
>
> *A day comes when an overqualified assistant becomes tired of picking up your laundry, managing your many girlfriends, lying to them, acting as your personal alarm clock, and a new low, even for you, Mr. Lord, bringing you a cold bottle of water at the end of your run. You run? When did you start running?*
>
> *Never mind.*
>
> *Oh… I almost forgot, having me stalk your brother and his fiancée that was not your finest moment and actually lower than the water thing. (Delete—maybe.)*
>
> *The point is, yes, the money is excellent,*

but you are not (Remember to revise). I quit. This is my two-weeks' notice.

Not Even Sincerely, (Remember to delete)
Delilah O'Shay

My jaw drops. "What the hell did I just read."

"Is everything okay, Orion?" Cab asks.

I rub the side of my face, trying to finish absorbing what I just read. "No, Cab. Everything is definitely not okay."

The next book in The Lords of Manhattan series is *Boss On Notice*; it will be released on August 2, 2022.

PRE-ORDER TODAY

Made in United States
Orlando, FL
04 April 2022

16484637R00209